Books by Crissy Smith

Were Chronicles

Pack Alpha
Pack Enforcer
Pack Territory
Pack Community
Pack Rogue
Pack Mates
Pack Daughter
Pack Hunter
Pack Council
Pack Security
Pack Beta
Pack Secrets
Pack Balance
Pack Investigator
Pack Law

Corporate Wolves

The Favour
Losing Control

Secrets

The Shifter and the Dreamer

Shifter Chronicles

Birds of Prey
Bear Claw
Eye of the Tiger

Coyote's Kiss
Wolf Pack

Bloodlines

Bite
Control

Bite Me!

Savage Love

Summer Seductions

Summers' Girl

Cloaks and Daggers

Vampire Hunter

Lust Bites

Seduced by the Neighbour
Fated Love
Bid High
Lacey's Seduction

What's Her Secret?

What's Her Secret?
Designated Alpha
Last Call

Single Titles

Eternal
Magical Ménage
Pack Rogue

Vamps in the City
Pack Community

Control

ISBN # 978-1-78686-106-1

©Copyright Crissy Smith 2017

Cover Art by Posh Gosh ©Copyright 2017

Interior text design by Claire Siemaszkiewicz

Totally Bound Publishing

Published in 2017 by Totally Bound Publishing, Newland House, The Point, Weaver Road, Lincoln, LN6 3QN, United Kingdom.

Bloodlines

CONTROL

CRISSY SMITH

Dedication

For all my readers. Embrace who you are and never let anyone else control your dreams.

Chapter One

Kieran Smith parked his brand new Harley two blocks up on Falcon Ave from the Murphy Institute before jogging toward the building. Anyone else who walked by wouldn't think there was anything weird about the normal-looking place, but inside an entire division of supernatural people worked tirelessly to save the world from the paranormal creatures that would harm them. Or protected the mystical citizens from the humans that hunted *them* for far worse reasons. The reason Kieran had gotten involved with them in the first place.

As a highly trained agent for the secret agency, the Organization, Kieran could just walk in through the front door if he wanted. Instead, he stopped right outside the line of sight of the guardhouse. The building had underground parking for their agents, but everyone had to be authorized to get in. Or at least they were supposed to be. Kieran had other plans.

Spotting the familiar figure inside the tiny house, Kieran grinned. His good old buddy Charlie. Actually, the little shifter was terrified of Kieran. Anytime Kieran drove by or was in the passenger seat of a vehicle, Charlie would hit the button to open the gates as fast as he could before scrambling away. The fear that wafted off Charlie would normally send Kieran's predator instincts through the roof, but luckily he had much more control than other Walkers. So he just enjoyed screwing with the man.

And maybe, just maybe, he'd flashed his fangs at the small shifter one too many times, but seriously, as an agent, Charlie should really be able to handle him.

"Let's have some fun," Kieran whispered to himself as he pressed back against a neighboring wall. Using the supernatural speed of his Day Walker genes, Kieran rushed right past the guard with only a dozen feet between them.

That was too easy. For an association that employed the best, brightest and most dangerous paranormal people, their security was really lacking. He'd already broken in once before. The first time he'd been in the place and still he'd gotten what he'd wanted. Of course, he'd also gotten caught. This time he had an even better plan. Kieran strolled casually across the parking garage, not worried about the cameras at all. Inside his pocket he fingered the little device he'd pressed as he'd gotten in. The cameras should now be playing an animated cartoon from Japan. That should give security a little shock. But that also meant he needed to hurry before they got off their lazy asses and investigated. Not that Kieran knew if they were lazy or not, but that was beside the point.

He hurried over to the shiny black SUV parked in the corner in one of the few reserved spots in the parking garage. The director, Marcello Sparro, had just gotten the new ride and Kieran was sure he would have a state-of-the-art alarm system. In fact, he was counting on it.

Kieran glanced around quickly. His senses told him he was alone, but he double-checked before he walked right up to the vehicle. He had to fight the temptation to see if he could break in without setting off the alarm. He was almost certain he could, but Kieran knew he was running out of time. Maybe he'd save that for another day when he wanted to piss off his new boss.

Instead Kieran began to rock the SUV back and forth. It only took until his second push to have the loud, piercing alarm blare. *Perfect.*

Kieran leapt away before he ran to the front again. He hid in the shadows as Charlie raced by him. *Just as planned.* Kieran rushed back to the guardhouse and grinned at seeing Charlie hadn't locked it behind him. He pushed the door open and grabbed the extra radio off the counter. Now he would be able to hear the communication between the agents. He turned the small device on and immediately picked up the chaotic chatter.

No one knew what was going on or who was responsible. Kieran backed out of the building before pressing the knob to lock it up. Since Charlie's keys were sitting next to the small television, the poor shifter wouldn't be able to get back in.

He felt a small twinge of regret but quickly pushed it away. He was doing this to show Charlie and all the other agents they had a lot more training to do. He'd seen so many holes in security and he was going to help plug them up. He just happened to be an asshole, so in his opinion the best way to show the company was to make everyone else feel like fucking idiots. Plus, anything that pissed off the director made Kieran happy.

Although he knew two people who would be mad at his latest stunt, since both his lover Dakota and his partner Remy had taken to not leaving him alone at the office in an attempt to make sure he was behaving properly. They'd both gotten busy earlier and he'd found himself driving to work by alone. Really, he could blame them for not keeping a better eye on him. He chuckled and thought about how that argument would play out.

The sound of running footsteps reached him, so Kieran knew he had to get a move on.

Kieran double-timed it to the stairwell he normally used. To move around inside the building, agents were required to use the elevators that were only operable with an authorized key card. That way the higher ups could track their agents. Kieran refused to use the elevators and on his first day there had disabled the stairway door monitors. They'd never been fixed.

Pounding up the stairs, he could hear agents scrambling around on their level even through the thick fire doors. His hearing was better than a shifter's, so he knew just where to go. This little experiment was turning out better than he could have hoped.

He reached the second floor and skittered to a stop. His partner, Remy, was leaning casually against the exit with his arms folded across his chest. Fuck, he had two more parts of his plan to carry out.

"*Really?*" Remy drawled.

"What? I just got here — what's going on?"

Remy snorted. "I watched your entire show."

"And you didn't interfere?" Kieran asked, surprised.

"I figured it would just be easier to let you do your thing. Just answer me one question."

"Okay," Kieran agreed. There was no telling what was going on in Remy's head. While his partner was trying to keep him out of trouble, he also helped him out from time to time.

"Why?"

"They need to tighten security. Just thought I'd help out."

"And you couldn't just send a report?"

"That's two questions," Kieran pointed out.

Remy pushed off the wall while shaking his head. "Come on, we got a call to take."

"But I want to watch them scramble around," Kieran whined.

"Do you *really* want to be here when Sparro finds out it was you who was responsible?"

"What makes you think he will? I never checked in tonight."

"Because no one else would be as stupid."

"I really don't think calling me stupid is nice," Kieran pouted.

"It's true, though." Remy slapped him on the back. "Now let's go."

Kieran knew his partner was right, but he'd really been looking forward to seeing the look on Director Sparro's face when he figured out what Kieran had done. It was petty, but since Kieran and Sparro's first meeting had ended with

Sparro besting him, Kieran was still looking for revenge.

The last month had been full of too many changes for Kieran and he blamed Sparro for most of them.

If Sparro hadn't allowed Kieran's real boss Caspar to take a dangerous undercover assignment, Kieran would still be working for Caspar and wouldn't be in this city in the first place. Plus, he wouldn't be struggling with his feelings for a certain sexy jaguar shifter. Of course, if he hadn't been transferred to Las Vegas, he wouldn't have met Dakota and, shifter or not, Kieran was pretty sure he was in love with her. Then there was the ghost from his past, the only man who had seen Kieran going through the darkest time of his life. Kieran and Jackson had a bond only two men who'd survived hell could form. If he hadn't landed in Vegas, Kieran would still believe his old friend dead.

So maybe the changes weren't all bad.

That was a thought for another day.

"Hurry," Remy called back over his shoulder. "We want to get away before anyone sees us."

"Hey, I'm waiting on you, fur ball," Kieran teased.

As expected, Remy growled before he sped up. They reached the ground floor and burst through the door into complete and utter chaos. Remy grabbed Kieran's arm and yanked him around a running agent and away. Remy pointed to one of the black SUVs the agents on shift used. Kieran hated the damn vehicles, preferring his bike, but Remy refused to ride with him. Something about a shifter not being able to survive a hundred-mile-an-hour crash no matter how easily he normally healed.

Remy ran over to the driver's side, so Kieran threw open the passenger door and jumped inside. Before Kieran even had his seat belt on, Remy was taking off. Kieran glanced behind him and grinned. No one had even been paying attention to them. He spotted Charlie in front of his guardhouse, trying to yank the door open. Kieran had created enough of a mess that he could hold off on the other pranks he had planned. It might even work out better, since

Sparro was sure to still be pissed for a while.

"Dakota is going to kick my ass," Remy muttered.

Kieran couldn't help but smile. His jaguar shifter was a force to be reckoned with and she was going to blame Remy for not watching Kieran better. Although he was sure she'd have a few choice words for him as well. Except Kieran knew how to distract his lover. So, while she might be mad, there was no way she'd stay so.

"You really should've picked me up on the way to the office."

"You're a grown fucking man!" Remy shouted. "I had to take a call from the local Alpha and be there early. It would have been just as bad if you'd been in the office for two hours longer than normal."

"That's a good point," Kieran agreed. "Maybe she won't be too upset with you."

His partner only glared at him before turning his attention back to the road. Kieran watched the scenery fly by as they headed away from the middle of the city. He preferred the less populated areas, but living in a hotel on the Strip, and with the office not far from it, he always seemed to be surrounded by people. He hated people.

"What did the Alpha want?" Kieran asked. Remy was a wolf shifter, but he didn't belong to the local Pack. Instead, he remained bonded to his birth Pack, which was made up of his family. It was rare for an Organization agent to have contact with family, but Remy's relatives were different. Kieran loved that his best friend still had that connection. Even if he was a little envious.

"Another Pack member disappeared," Remy told him.

"Shit!" That was the second wolf and fourth shifter total that had gone missing in the past month and a half. From what Kieran could piece together, the disappearances had started right before he'd gotten into town. Remy and he had only been looking into them for the past two weeks, though. The other agents that had been in charge of the case had been reassigned when the Alpha refused to work with them. It had taken some digging around, or bribing the hacker from his old division, to find out what had happened.

Instead of looking for the wolf shifter that had never returned to the Pack house, the agents had been stopping in at strip joints and spending their money on booze and women. The Alpha, frustrated at the lack of progress, had ordered the agents followed by some of his enforcers and they'd reported back their findings to the Alpha.

Kieran would have loved to have been a fly in the wall when the Alpha had shown up at their office and screamed at Sparro. From what the gossip mill shared, Sparro and the Alpha had almost come to blows. But when things had finally calmed down, the two agents had been suspended and sent somewhere like Alaska while Remy and Kieran had taken over the search.

Remy being a wolf shifter had helped calm the Alpha. And since Kieran never met with any of the shifters, neither of them had to worry about Kieran pissing the Alpha off.

Leaving Remy in charge of all contact worked best for them.

"The file's in the back seat," Remy said.

Kieran reached out and grabbed the manila folder lying in the back of the car. It had grown thick in the past few weeks while Kieran and Remy had added notes as they'd investigated. Every night for fourteen nights they'd been trying to find a link between the three, now four shifters that had disappeared, and had already gathered more information than the first idiot agents.

"Where are we headed?" he asked as he opened the folder.

"The tunnels. Last place the wolf, Max, was seen," Remy informed him.

Max Webb was twenty-seven years old, dark-haired and hazel-eyed. A reporter for one of the local news stations, he'd been interviewing some of the tunnel people when he hadn't returned to work or the territory. Kieran would have suspected someone hadn't liked Max looking into the very quiet, secretive community of the tunnel people, but with other shifters missing, all avenues would have to be investigated.

"We're meeting with the guy the Alpha said was the last to speak to Max," Remy said.

"That can't be good."

"The Alpha vouched for him. Stated he was being cooperative and wanted to help Max."

Kieran snorted. The Alpha had probably applied some pressure to get that promise. Even *he'd* heard the local Alpha was sort of a badass. Kieran would never give much credit to a shifter, but from what he'd heard about the Alpha, Damon, even Kieran could admit the man did a damn good job of running a Pack.

"Just let me do the talking to this guy," Remy requested.

Kieran shrugged. Didn't matter to him. "Just park far enough away that we can check out the area first." It might be Remy's job to handle interviews, but Kieran would make sure his partner was safe. "This isn't the kind of place we want to be strolling around in the dark."

"Okay," Remy agreed easily.

The farther away from the busy tourist roads they got, the more Kieran felt at home. If he had his choice, he'd spend all his time outdoors, like he'd used to when he first started with the Organization.

In the old days, he'd be going up and down the streets and alleys, hoping to come across a paranormal creating trouble. Now there was a lot more investigating than there'd ever been before. Kieran was still hunting late at night or when no one else knew. Actually, both Remy and Dakota probably knew Kieran didn't just *come* across the situations that led him to call for a car to pick up suspects he'd taken down. Neither said anything to him, and he didn't think they would unless he got hurt. And that wasn't going to happen.

Remy pulled off to the side of the road and Kieran peered down at the drainage ditch and tunnels beyond. There didn't seem to be anyone around, but he was still cautious when it came to his partner.

"Ready?" Remy asked.

"Where you meeting this guy?" Kieran questioned as he climbed out of the SUV.

"At the entrance. He's sort of nervous about talking to me."

"He should be," Kieran muttered. He really didn't like this. His gut was screaming at him that he and Remy were walking into a trap.

"Just go." Remy waved him on.

The shadows deepened the closer Kieran and Remy got to the entrance of the tunnels. When Kieran had first arrived in Las Vegas, he'd had no idea there was an entire underground community beneath the city. Now he was more familiar with the area, he knew the dangers that lurked around him. He'd only been there once before, when he'd been tracking a thief who was a shifter and hiding out. The residents had been wary of him, but when Kieran had only taken his suspect and left them alone, they'd disappeared without trying to stop him. Kieran was thankful for that. He might be an asshole, but he never hurt innocents.

Still, coming down here again made Kieran nervous. Sure, most of the homeless people were harmless, but not all of them. There would always be an element of society that would abuse and take advantage of the less fortunate. Those types thrived in this environment.

"Are you sure about this contact?" Kieran asked his partner. Remy had great instincts when it came to investigating cases, which was why he was always the one to communicate with witnesses or potential suspects. In the past, when they'd worked with Angel as their third partner, Kieran hadn't been brought in until Remy and Angel were ready to take down the bad guy.

But with the recent changes, he and Remy were now working in a new city, under a new boss, and Kieran served as Remy's backup all the time. It wasn't how Kieran liked to work, but for the moment he was playing nice. Or, at least, making it appear so. If his little prank earlier didn't get him on Sparro's shit list, Kieran didn't know what would.

He was pressing his luck, but he needed to know how Sparro would handle him. Plus, he really did want the building Remy and Dakota worked in to be safe. He would not let anything happen to the two of them. So, while he was having some fun, there was a purpose behind it. He didn't trust their safety to anyone but himself.

Kieran had trust issues, but after ten years of torture at the hands of shifters, that had to be expected. The other agents in the Organization avoided him at all costs, but Remy and Dakota had his back. Them, he trusted. Sparro and the others had yet to prove themselves to Kieran.

"Remy! Are you sure your contact is coming?" Kieran was getting a really bad feeling.

Remy shrugged, which really didn't make Kieran feel any better. "He called the local Alpha, who passed on the message to us. The only time he could meet with us tonight was now. He's a shifter also, so he should want to help us."

Kieran grunted in response. He couldn't tell Remy they'd probably be better off with fewer shifters in general. As much as he hated shifters, he found himself caring about a few of them, and that was fucking with his head.

"I know what you're thinking," Remy claimed as he waved a finger in Kieran's face.

"Stop it." Kieran smacked Remy's hand away.

"Damn, I can't believe you're still so grumpy. I would have guessed getting laid regularly improved your disposition," Remy bitched.

Instead of answering, Kieran peered around him. It was best not to encourage Remy when he brought up Dakota. Kieran's partner loved the fact that after years of attempting to forget shifters even existed, Kieran was now living with one. Better to just focus on what had brought them out here in the middle of the night.

He could just make out the opening to the two tunnels

that were supposed to be empty. This time of night, when the creatures came out to hunt, the tunnel people had worked out a safety program to watch out for one another. Kieran had discreetly kept an eye on them and found the people who lived there were very smart. So Kieran knew they were deep back, protected by traps they'd set. But even though Kieran expected them to be hidden, there was still an eerie feel around him.

It was weird how quiet it was. Even with his superior hearing, Kieran didn't pick up the usual sounds that would echo around the abandoned area. He motioned to Remy, so his partner would stop giving him a hard time and pay attention. Remy did a little stutter step before nodding. Maybe Kieran wasn't the only one feeling uneasy.

When Remy tilted his head up and sniffed, Kieran swiftly moved to press back to back with him. Years of having worked together in dangerous situations made it easy for him to anticipate what his partner would need. In the event Remy needed to shift, Kieran literally had his back.

"Something's coming," Remy whispered.

Kieran already knew that, so he didn't bother to respond. He'd just picked up the faint sound of footsteps. He turned his head then narrowed his eyes and concentrated his gaze on the entrance to the right tunnel. The echoes seemed to be loud in the quiet, dark night, but Kieran knew very few would be able to pick them up like he and Remy could.

He took a deep breath, but all he could smell was the stink of body odor and old blood. Remy was already growling, which made the hair on the back of Kieran's neck stand up.

"Do we attack?" Remy asked in a low murmur.

"Wait," Kieran cautioned. While the situation didn't feel normal, they couldn't risk the chance of whoever was exiting the tunnels being human.

It didn't take long for the shape of a man to appear, but Kieran knew right away this wasn't a normal human. Neither was the person the figure was carrying.

"Stop!" Kieran ordered in his most commanding voice.

The figure stopped just outside the tunnel entrance. It was easier to see it was a young man, even with the black hoodie over his head and clenched tight around his face. But enough was visible. In his arms was the body of a small woman. Kieran couldn't determine age, but he could see the female was at least still breathing.

"Put her down," Kieran shouted. "Now!"

"I can't," the younger shifter called back. "I have to take them another one."

"Keep his attention," Remy whispered. "I'll try to edge closer."

"Be careful," Kieran murmured. "He's a bear shifter."

"He's also scared to death," Remy replied. "He doesn't want to hurt anyone."

"We can help you," Kieran told the bear shifter. "Just put her down and let us help you."

"No," the newcomer cried. "No one can. I'm in too deep now."

Kieran relaxed his stance, certain, even though he didn't know exactly what this kid was talking about, they could take care of this without violence. The more the bear shifter spoke, the more Kieran was certain he was young, no more than twenty, and Remy was right—he was scared. Kieran was sure this guy was involved with the missing shifters.

"Listen to me," Kieran ordered. "It's not too late."

The kid laughed then. Threw his head back and howled. "Too late? It is for me and now for you too. We're all screwed."

A growl came from behind him and Kieran spun right before he was knocked back. He caught his balance then launched himself at his two attackers. They were shifters and one smelt like a feline, but Kieran couldn't place the other right away. It didn't matter though. A Day Walker going up against shifters? The Walker would win every time, even if the two teamed up, which only the smart did. It would take at least four to bring him down. He took them both to the ground, but the feline was instantly back up.

The feline's eyes widened as Kieran bared his teeth. He actually took a step back. Yeah, they hadn't known he was a Walker. Probably pegged him as just being human. That had been a mistake.

Instead of giving up like Kieran had hoped, the feline crouched then leapt.

Kieran didn't have time to check on Remy, but he could hear the battle going on behind him, and his partner's grunt. Oh, this was fucking bullshit. They'd either been set up or had gotten lucky enough to see a shifter snatching up close and personal. Either way, these assholes were not going to get away with another victim.

"Fucker," Kieran snarled when the feline managed to land a hard punch to Kieran's jaw. Kieran drew back his arm and landed three quick jabs to the man's temple, which took him out. He turned then crouched as the other shifter jumped at him. Kieran caught him by his neck and held him up with his legs dangling. Damn, a horse shifter. That species was strong, but they were also slow.

"Who are you working for?" Kieran asked as he tightened his grip.

"Not telling you!" the horse shifter spat.

Kieran yanked him close and let his eyes glow. Anyone who knew anything about Walkers would know about feeding.

"Shit! Get off me, you freak." The horse shifter tried to claw at Kieran's hand.

"Who are you working for?" Kieran repeated.

"You'll find out soon enough," the horse shifter replied. He grinned then kicked Kieran in the nuts.

"Fuck!" Kieran roared as his grip on his opponent loosened and he dropped to his knees. Yep, no matter the species of man, a solid kick in the balls was a good move. Kieran was used to real fighters and not elementary antics.

Before Kieran could recover, his feet were swept out from under him and he fell, hard. As he landed, his suspect leapt over him and ran toward the other fight involving Remy.

Kieran rolled up onto his feet as he searched for the horse.

Remy was holding his own against what appeared to be yet another shifter. At least the bear shifter seemed to be down and the woman safely tucked into the entrance of the tunnels.

"Rem!" Kieran called in warning.

His partner ducked just in time to avoid a blow to the back of his head. Kieran yelled before he launched himself toward the group. The shifters scrambled away and started to run. Instead of following after them, Kieran went to his partner's aid. Remy's head was bleeding pretty badly. Kieran had no trouble fighting his urge for the liquid his body craved. When it came to his partner, the sight of Remy's blood was enough to make him feel sick.

"I'm okay." Remy waved him off. "Go check on the girl."

Kieran made sure Remy's wound was already closing up before he agreed. "All right, stay here." He patted Remy on the back before he rushed to the tunnel entrance. Kieran wasn't surprised when Remy pushed himself up off the ground and started to follow him.

The woman, an owl shifter by her scent, was still knocked out. Kieran bent and sniffed. They must have given her something to put her to sleep. He could pick up the faint trace of metal and saline. An odor that threatened to finish off his stomach and have him vomiting.

The memories, dark and scary, that went along with that scent had his head spinning and Kieran had to clench his teeth to fight to remain in control. As he breathed deeply, he kept his eyes open. He was afraid if he closed them, flashes from his past would assault him.

Once the sensation passed, Kieran laid the woman flat on her back and took her wrist to monitor her pulse. "We need to call for an ambulance."

"And backup," Remy agreed as he stood and pulled out his phone. "I don't know what happened here, but this shit was fucked up. If we hadn't been here…"

"Yeah," Kieran replied. Remy didn't need to finish the

thought. Would someone have even reported the young woman missing? If she was living in the tunnels, there was a good chance the answer to that question would have been no. He hadn't really considered before how many shifters might not have been reported to the police as missing. It looked like their case had just gotten a whole lot more complicated.

He gazed down at the young woman. Her pulse was still steady, so that was good. She couldn't have been much older than the bear shifter who had tried to take her. What she was doing in the tunnels, he couldn't guess. Her high-priced jeans and shoes told him she didn't live down there. On the streets, no way would she have kept those items. If she hadn't been mugged for them, she could have sold them for money.

There had to be a connection between the tunnels and missing shifters. Kieran just needed to figure out what. He glanced up at his partner when he heard the soft footsteps.

"Backup and ambulance should be here soon," Remy said. He crouched down while shaking his head. "She's young, just like the others."

Kieran peered around. "Now what?" he asked. There was no sign of anyone else, but he could hear a few people had come close to the tunnel entrance.

"Now, we'll get some agents down here to question potential witnesses," Remy said.

"No one is going to talk to us."

"I know. We have to try, though. Once we're done here, I'll go see the Alpha and try to get more out of him about this call that brought us down. I have a feeling he didn't tell me everything."

"I'm going with you," Kieran demanded. He might not like dealing with shifters, but this was different.

"Oh no, you're not."

Kieran glared. "Yes, I am. He already set you up once."

"We don't know that. We're lucky the Alpha even called us. He doesn't exactly trust us after what happened with the other agents."

Kieran couldn't believe what he was hearing. "And you just made my point. This could be payback."

"K, trust me." Remy glanced up so he could meet his gaze. "I need to do this on my own. I can't have you threatening the Alpha. This is our best chance to get answers on what happened here tonight."

"I won't threaten him," he promised. If it kept his partner safe, then Kieran would maintain a tight hold on his control.

"If I don't find out what I want, I'll start taking you with me. A face-to-face between the Alpha and me is all I'm asking for first," Remy insisted.

Kieran wanted to argue more, but he knew Remy had his mind made up. "You call me before you meet and as soon as you're done. One hour. If I don't hear from you in one hour, I will bust into that place and tear apart every shifter there."

Remy merely lifted a brow at him.

"I mean it," Kieran declared.

"Okay," Remy agreed as sirens and lights started to fill up the quiet space.

Kieran turned and saw some of their agents were the first to arrive. "I'm going to start the interviews. You deal with *them*." He waved his hand toward the approaching agents.

"Got it, partner."

Chapter Two

"Stupid, stupid, son of a bitch," Dakota Reese muttered as she slammed the door to the suite she and her lover were staying in. She dropped her keys onto the long glossy table next to the entry before she stomped to the bedroom. A mere month, thirty days only, was how long the man she was dating had been at the local branch of the Organization and he'd managed to create complete chaos every time her back was turned.

Kieran was such an odd mixture of charming yet sarcastic that he made work more interesting. His harmless insults and pokes at other agents were one thing, but he'd obviously gotten bored and more imaginative tonight.

If she wasn't almost sure she loved the guy, Dakota would be very tempted to rip out his throat. As hard as she'd tried to figure out why he would pull a stunt like that, she just couldn't understand.

And this was all before she found out he'd been attacked earlier! From what other agents had told her, Kieran and Remy had been investigating the missing shifters and had a meeting with a witness. Then all hell had broken loose and they'd stopped a girl from being abducted. Of course a fight had taken place since it was Kieran. All she could think about was instead of being able to check on him, she'd been sitting in their boss's office getting reamed out because Kieran had decided to screw with the other agents.

She was furious.

As she reached the threshold of the bedroom, Kieran came out of the bathroom, towel drying his long black hair. Dakota braced her feet shoulder-width apart and fisted her hands on her hips. "Really?" she asked in a tone that would usually put fear into her suspects.

Kieran glanced up and grinned. "You're home early."

She narrowed her eyes while pressing her lips together. She would not laugh. Would not give him the satisfaction of knowing he amused her deep down with his childish antics. He could have been seriously hurt while she had been getting screamed at. "And why am I back early?" she drawled.

"Because you missed me?" he asked with innocence lacing his words.

Dakota knew better. "Try again."

"Something wrong, love?" he inquired, strolling forward.

Thank God Kieran had put on a robe after his shower, was all Dakota could think as he made his way slowly toward her. If he'd been naked, she wouldn't have been able to resist him at all. How he could be so fucking hot and annoying at the same time was a mystery.

She took a deep breath before pointing a finger at him. "Why?" she asked. "What would you gain from breaking into the office...again?"

Kieran laughed, his bright blue eyes sparkling. "Technically I didn't break into the office. Plus, I did warn Charlie he should keep a better eye out. It's not my fault he didn't see me enter."

"Sparro's new vehicle?" she asked because she just had to know why.

Kieran shrugged. "Just testing his alarm for him."

"Testing his alarm," she repeated. It was like talking to a child sometimes. "Do you know how pissed he is? And what about the cartoons on the security feed?"

"You forgot to mention locking Charlie out of his own guardhouse. I really liked that touch."

Dakota sighed. "It took them three hours to get everything sorted out and to determine there wasn't a threat."

"I'm sorry I missed that. Remy made me leave before I could really enjoy the show."

"How'd you get by him to pull your little stunt?" Usually Remy helped her keep Kieran under wraps and with her out of the office, it had been up to Remy to distract Kieran.

"I tossed a ball and told him to fetch," Kieran replied in a flat tone. He didn't even smile.

"Funny," Dakota deadpanned

"If you're nice to me, I'll give you the ball of string I bought you," he teased.

Dakota smiled, right before she balled her fist and punched him in the stomach. Because of her shifter strength, she pulled her hit some to ensure she didn't really hurt him. Not that it was ever easy to injure a Walker. Still, there were times she wished she could go full jaguar on him. But she knew that would be the fastest way to really lose him.

Kieran grunted then wrapped his arms around her and yanked her off her feet.

She squeaked before his mouth landed on hers and he kissed her.

Damn it, how was she supposed to stay mad at him when his touch made her feel more alive than ever before? Passion swept over her as Kieran nibbled on her bottom lip while sliding his hands up to cup her butt.

She wrapped her legs around his waist before she arched against him, pressing her chest against his. It had only been a little over twelve hours since they'd left each other after beginning their morning with a passionate bout of lovemaking, and still she felt as if she'd burn up from the inside.

"You aren't really mad, are you?" Kieran asked as their lips parted.

"Yes, I had to sit and listen for thirty minutes as Sparro ranted about what you did," Dakota told him. "Thirty minutes!"

Kieran placed his mouth against her neck, but she knew he was smiling. "I'm really sorry about that."

"Liar," Dakota said fondly. She wasn't mad at him, but he didn't need to know that. "Now let me down."

"And if I don't? You going to hit me again?"

"I might. This time in that pretty face of yours."

Kieran leaned his head back so their gazes met. "But you like my pretty face."

She did. "And yet sometimes I have the urge to put my fist through it."

He barked out a laugh, then finally put her back on her feet. Dakota pushed away from him before she could get distracted by his touch again.

"On top of having to listen to the lecture meant for you, I find out you were attacked tonight!" she exclaimed.

Kieran grew serious. "I'm okay."

"*Okay?*" she repeated. "From what I hear, there were four shifters."

"And Remy was with me."

"Four shifters, Kieran!"

"They were easily taken care of. The day I can't take out a couple shifters is the day I—"

"You really don't want to finish that," she warned as she walked past him, farther into the bedroom they'd been sharing for the last few weeks. Housekeeping had been by earlier, so the bed was made with fresh sheets and blankets. She inhaled the clean scent before continuing to the bathroom. She loved the bathroom.

When Kieran had first gotten to town, he'd rented a smaller room inside the hotel-casino. But since Kieran's oldest friend owned the place, Jackson had been able to talk Kieran into moving into a bigger suite with a kitchen. Dakota had liked the other, but this one was pure decadence.

Even though she still had her own room at the Organization housing building, Dakota was finding herself at Kieran's more and more. The hot sex wasn't the only reason she kept returning either.

Her hands shook as she braced them against the marble vanity. It was common for Kieran to make remarks about his feelings on shifters. She'd grown used to them for the most part, but sometimes it still hurt.

He had every right to feel the way he did after being tortured for ten years, but other than her and Remy, Kieran couldn't stand being around any other shifters. It made her worry about their future.

"I'm sorry."

She glanced up into the mirror and saw him braced against the bathroom door, watching her. She smiled. "I know what you mean, but sometimes…" She let her words trail off, not having the courage to bring up the familiar fight.

Deep down she knew Kieran didn't think before he spoke most of the time. He wasn't trying to hurt her. In the privacy of their home, the elegant hotel suite, Kieran showed her a part of him no one else got to see.

No one would ever believe it, but Kieran was a nester. He enjoyed high-end items, luxury and soft fabrics. Their bed was always piled high with an excessive amount of pillows and blankets. Even though Kieran's body temperature was colder than hers, that wasn't the only reason for the extra layers. Kieran was a snuggler as well.

Growing up in the Organization training facilities hadn't given Dakota the chance to take advantage of the luxuries available to others. Kieran had changed that for her. He made sure she could have whatever she wanted. He shared the small lavish comforts he enjoyed. He also indulged in the best food and drink, making sure she was always included. He might seem like a bad-boy biker, but really he was someone who loved extravagance.

She glanced over her shoulder, admiring his body. "Shame you already showered."

Kieran growled before he stepped closer. She smiled then pushed against his chest, shoving him back before she slammed the door closed. She locked it for good measure.

They both knew she wasn't angry, but if she made him wait just a little bit, Kieran would no doubt make her pay later. A shiver of arousal and need traveled up her spine. Tonight should be fun.

They might have only been sleeping together for a month, but the connection between the two of them was strong. From the moment she'd seen Kieran standing in a dark, dirty alley, she'd known he was the man she was supposed to be with. Kieran had gone back and forth between wanting her with every fiber of his being and trying to push her away. It still surprised her sometimes that they were together. With her jaguar always close to the surface, Dakota worried she'd scare him away one day. Kieran remained cautious anytime he could sense her animal, but he'd also accepted her in his life. Still, their relationship was always teetering on a ledge.

There was still steam in the air and Dakota didn't wait to turn on the shower and add to it. There were four faucet heads inside the glass and marble stall. Four! She'd never been big on water play while in her shifted form, but one day when she knew Kieran wouldn't accidently stumble in on her, she was going to transform and let her jaguar have some fun.

With quick and efficient movements, she undressed before stepping under the hot spray. She didn't even attempt to hold in her moan of pleasure. While Kieran had been playing around in the office, she had been trying to run down a confidential informant. The little fox shifter usually gave her the best intel, but now, when Dakota needed him the most, Jerry had gone into hiding.

It was upsetting and as much as she wanted to think he was okay, her instincts told her differently. She was aware of the case Kieran and Remy were working, plus she worried Jerry had gotten caught giving out information to cops or herself. Usually, he wasn't too difficult to find.

Shaking away the disturbing thoughts, Dakota began to wash the long day down the drain. She hadn't been kidding when she'd been bitching to Kieran about his prank. Funny — yes, the stunt had been funny, but the other agents were getting more and more pissed off at him. Not that Kieran seemed to care. He spoke to her and Remy and no one else. Even the director had trouble getting Kieran to say two words to him.

Although she'd brought up him hanging out more with others, Kieran only scoffed at her. She'd known he was a loner when they met and there wasn't anything she could think of that would change that fact, but she was trying. She was hoping if he began to feel at home in her city, then maybe he would stay, even after his boss came off assignment. They didn't talk about the future, so all Dakota could do was worry and hope.

Kieran living in the hotel was just another reminder he hadn't put down roots. She understood it was easier and cheaper to be there, thanks to Kieran's old friend's generosity. It also gave Jackson and Kieran the chance to reconnect.

They'd been together years before as victims of the shifters that had taken them. When Jackson had been taken out of the cell and had never returned, Kieran had believed him dead.

Now not only was Jackson alive, but the two men were closer than ever before. Jackson still appeared uncomfortable around her, though. Just like Kieran, Jackson didn't like to be around shifters. It made it hard for her to get to know her lover's friend.

As she rubbed shampoo into her hair, she heard the soft click of the bathroom door closing. She didn't even try to hide her smile. Of course he'd managed to get the locked door open and followed her. Kieran loved seeing her wet and slippery, as he'd told her time and time again.

"I thought I told you not to come in here," she said even though she didn't mean it.

"I'm just here to make sure you get clean. Your health is very important to me," Kieran responded as he opened the glass stall door.

Dakota wiped the water from her eyes. "I'm clean. Thanks for the offer, though."

"No," Kieran said while still moving closer. "You missed

a spot."

She smirked. "Really?"

"Right here," Kieran said right before he leaned down and ran his tongue in the shell of her ear.

She shivered and tried to push him away. "Stop. I'm still mad at you."

Kieran moved behind her, running his hands over her body the entire time. Even through the hot water and steam, goosebumps rose.

"No you're not," he whispered knowingly.

"K…"

"I'm really sorry you got yelled at for me," he whispered. "But I think when I turn in my suggestions on how we can approve security, you'll be impressed."

Dakota sighed. "There are better ways to make changes you think we need. If you would just send in a report, almost every agent in that place would not only read it but would agree."

"Then what would I get out of that?" He actually sounded genuinely confused.

She turned in his arms before she palmed his face in her hands. "You're a brilliant man and I don't want to see Sparro strangle you in front of my eyes."

"Like he could."

"I mean it."

He shrugged. "Like I care what anyone thinks of me. If Sparro doesn't like it, he can fire me."

There was no reasoning with him when Kieran got in this mood. And Kieran did have other options. Jackson had offered more than once to hire Kieran to run one of his security companies anywhere in the world. If he wanted, Kieran could travel and see places she'd only dreamed about. Kieran didn't seem interested in the job, but that didn't mean if Sparro pissed him off enough, Kieran wouldn't take Jackson up on his offer.

If that happened, Dakota would end up not only losing Kieran at work, but probably also in all aspects of her life.

"Okay, I might not be mad at you, but that doesn't mean I'm in the mood," she said.

"How about if I do this…?" Kieran lowered his mouth to hers.

God, he tasted so good. Like caramel and spice. She groaned while wrapping her arms around his neck and pulling him close. His hands were slick as they brushed her thighs before he easily lifted her off her feet.

Her back hit the wall and she wrapped her legs around his hips. His cock, full and hard, nudged at her entrance. He was so strong, her Walker—she didn't have to worry about him dropping her.

"I missed you," Kieran said as he kissed along her neck.

She closed her eyes. Sometimes he could surprise her with sweet words like that. His tone would change to soft and loving and Dakota would forget all about the problems between them. "Me too."

"I'd do anything to keep you safe," he murmured. "Even if that means showing all the dumbass agents you work with they're morons."

"Was that what today's prank was about?"

He just grunted.

Dakota tightened her legs before she began rubbing up against him. Her nipples dragged along his smooth chest, making her stomach clench.

"Mm," he hummed in response.

"Inside me," she pleaded. "I want to feel you."

"What if I want to play?" he teased, running her hands up and down her thighs.

"Later, I promise."

His hand brushed against her as he gripped his cock. It wasn't long before the tip of his shaft was at her entrance. He began to press hard and her body opened for him like it always did. The hot, hard cock claiming her from the inside. Since they didn't have to worry about pregnancy, he didn't use a condom. They couldn't pass on diseases to each other with their paranormal genes.

Unlike in Hollywood movies, Kieran wasn't a vampire, dead or undead, but a living soul that had extraordinary gifts. He also had a rare disease that made drinking blood a part of his life.

Still, she loved that there was no barrier between them. He thrust deep, scattering all thoughts of disease, pregnancy and blood from her thoughts.

She dug her nails into his back, feeling the scars. He didn't like her to touch them, but to Dakota they were a sign he had survived. He was alive and with her.

"Feel me inside you," he murmured. "My body taking yours. You belong to me."

"Yes," she hissed. Her heart, body and soul were all his. Every part of her was tailored for this complicated man.

He drew back and gazed into her eyes as he plunged over and over, harder and faster. "Mine."

His blue eyes began to glow. "Always."

She held on as he slammed into her. She loved when he lost control. She was no fragile female. She was tough and a good pounding was what she craved. For her lover to prove he could not only handle her but give her a rough fuck too was something she had only gotten with him.

"More!" she demanded.

He snarled, his fangs dropping, but she wasn't afraid. Kieran would never bite her during sex. That was the very first rule he'd given her. Still, she loved when he came close.

"Show me. Show me how much you want me."

Kieran kept thrusting as Dakota ran her tongue across his neck. She loved the taste of him. Kieran might not hold scent in his skin but he did have his own unique flavor. When she reached the hard muscle where his neck and shoulder met, she bit down, making sure she didn't break the skin. She did so just because she could.

He growled then groaned as he hiked her farther up the wall so he could get a better angle, pushing his cock into her wet pussy. Each time he drove in hard, her back slammed against the surface behind her. As she began to tremble,

Dakota knew she wouldn't last much longer. Her breasts felt fuller and her clit began to tingle. She clawed at Kieran's back, which spurred him on further. His movements were so fast she could barely follow them, so she closed her eyes. He loosed a grunt as sweat dripped down his forehead. Dakota threw back her head as she screamed out her orgasm.

He didn't slow until his plunges grew frantic and he shouted as his own climax was ripped from him.

The quiet of the bathroom, just the sound of the water beating down on the tiles, wrapped around her as she lowered her forehead to his and closed her eyes in exhaustion.

* * * *

Kieran lifted his head and peered down at Dakota, who was still sleeping peacefully. She was truly beautiful. At times like this, he couldn't believe how lucky he was. After years of torture and abuse at the hands of monsters, Kieran had thought his life was over. He'd actually prayed nightly his pain would end. Instead, he'd been found by the Organization. And years later, even when he'd thought he was happy alone, he'd stumbled across Dakota.

She had fought for him, even gone up against Kieran's own fears to be with him. He didn't deserve her. He was fully aware of that, but, as long as she wanted him, Kieran would do everything in his power to make her happy.

He pressed a kiss to her forehead then, as carefully as he could, pulled out his arm from under her neck before he slid away. Luckily Dakota merely rolled over onto her stomach, still breathing deeply and softly.

Kieran climbed out of bed. He had to fight to keep the old memories at bay. Ever since he'd seen Jackson again, sleep had been hard for him. The nightmares he'd thought he'd escaped were back. Still, they were better than the flashbacks he was having. He was managing to keep his issues from Dakota, but he wasn't sure how long that would last. She was a smart girl and had great instincts — if he didn't figure out how to get rid of the nightmares or flashbacks, she would find out.

With the stealth of a Walker, Kieran crept to the chair where he'd left his sweat pants and long-sleeved T-shirt. Dakota ran hotter than he did, so Kieran was trying to get used to keeping his suite cooler than he preferred. Kieran closed the door behind him quietly. He dressed quickly right outside the bedroom door before heading into the main room. He heard a soft *ding* and strolled to his desk, where he'd plugged in his cell to charge. He clicked on the small lamp before picking up the phone.

Can we talk?

The text from Jackson had arrived two hours ago. Jackson was probably asleep by now, but Kieran typed back a message.

Yes, when?

He set down the phone before lifting the lid of his laptop and powering it up. If he wasn't going to be able to get any sleep, at least he would be able to check on his boss.

Kieran logged on to the Organization network, having to key in his password three different times before he was finally able to pull up the database where he and agents from his old division were tracking Caspar Westbridge.

Caspar had rescued Kieran on that cold night years ago from the cell deep inside Mount Fauna. He'd tracked his ex-partner and former best friend after the Organization had discovered Bradley Johnson had been kidnapping Day Walkers and experimenting on them, trying to figure out how to make the shifters live longer. Kieran didn't remember everything that had been done to him, but what he did know was all bad.

Bradley had wanted eternal life and the closest he'd been

able to find was the Walkers. They weren't immortal, but they did live longer than any other creatures. Bradley had been vicious in his pursuit, not caring how many Walkers he'd killed or hurt. Ten years Kieran had been tortured for the amusement and experiment of the shifters who'd held him.

Until he'd been saved.

Even though Caspar took Kieran home with him, it had taken months before Caspar could be around him without Kieran trying to attack, but eventually, through Caspar's kindness and understanding, Kieran had stopped being the monster the shifters had made him into and had started to trust his rescuer.

Through training, Caspar had taught Kieran to defend himself and become strong again. When Kieran had been ready, Caspar had broken every Organization rule by bringing Kieran into the fold. Kieran might have a lot of issues still, but he did believe in protecting those weaker than him. He knew he would spend the rest of his life in debt to Caspar.

So when his boss, the man he respected more than any other, his father figure, had taken an assignment after Bradley had surfaced again, Kieran had been truly afraid. If anything happened to Caspar, Kieran wasn't sure he would ever recover, even with Remy and Dakota by his side.

Luckily, Caspar had worked things out so Kieran could follow his progress. Kieran had access to the reports Caspar was sending in and could follow along with the investigation. He could also email Caspar his own thoughts and suggestions. Hell, even Dakota and Remy had started following along and giving their own ideas.

Kieran felt his pulse pick up when he saw Caspar had recently uploaded a video file. If Caspar was still giving updates, then he was still alive and well. At least that was one less worry for the night.

His phone dinged before he could open the file. He picked it up.

6 a.m. work?

He answered quickly. *Yes.*

I'll come to you.

Okay.

Kieran put down his phone again after replying. He was glad Jackson was willing to come to his suite. They could have met in Jackson's office or his own living quarters, but Kieran was hoping Jackson would grow more comfortable with Dakota. She was everything to him and it was important the two of them got along. Remy already loved her, so if Jackson would start to trust her, then his small circle would be complete.

Kieran glanced up to make sure she was still asleep, and smiled. Her soft breaths wouldn't be heard by a human ear, but he could easily pick up the sound. Satisfied she was where she belonged, Kieran double-clicked the video file and pulled it up before he pressed Play.

It appeared to be a recording from a phone. He jerked when Caspar's voice sounded.

"This is the latest lab we found," Caspar said. "We followed the trail to some caves in Arizona. Whoever was here had gone by the time we arrived. I don't know if they were tipped off we were coming or if they just had a feeling. It's obvious they haven't been gone long, though."

The camera panned, showing a concrete room with metal tables lined up. Kieran shivered. It was too much like the room they used to take him to.

"There were no living persons to rescue. We did find one dead Walker, though," Caspar continued. "The evidence shows the Walker had been dead almost a week. I've called for a team to pick up the body to try to figure out the cause of death. The computers were all wiped, but hopefully we can recover some data. We haven't been able to on the others, so I just don't know."

Kieran didn't like how defeated his boss sounded.

"I'm not sure where to go from here," Caspar said. "We started on the east coast and seem to be working our way back west. I'm almost certain Bradley is aware we're hunting him."

"Fuck," Kieran whispered. He balled his fist to keep from pounding the table. He wanted to be with his boss. He knew Caspar had a team he was working with, but Kieran didn't trust them to keep him safe. If Bradley knew Caspar was stalking him, there was no way of telling what the sadistic shifter would do to him.

Caspar was human. And, even though he was thoroughly trained, he wouldn't be much of a match against Bradley. Caspar had been out of the field for too damn long.

Even though Kieran would have a hard time dealing with the places Caspar was coming across, it would be better than watching from the wings. Waiting for something bad to happen.

"I'm moving from the lab to the holding cells," Caspar said. He entered a dark room and Kieran didn't want to see. He should turn the video off. He wouldn't, though.

Caspar flipped on the light and Kieran's stomach rolled. He closed his eyes, but he could still hear Caspar's voice explaining the room and the three cells.

He couldn't fight the memories that rushed forward.

He was cold, so damn cold. They had taken his clothes and left him lying naked and dirty on the metal bars. The entire cage was made up of steel poles. If he didn't move enough, the imprint of them would show on his body. He didn't have a blanket, a toilet – nothing. Just the fucking bars.

Kieran wrapped his hands around the rods in front of him.

What had he done to deserve this kind of treatment? He'd been traveling across country in his old pickup truck when he'd started having trouble with the stupid vehicle. It had been decades since the truck had seen better days, but Kieran still kept it maintained.

It should have gotten him to his destination. But as the truck sputtered, he managed to get it off the dark highway and onto the shoulder right before it died.

He'd popped the hood, but couldn't find the problem. He'd filled up only thirty miles ago, so he had plenty of gas. Still, the vehicle wasn't going anywhere.

Kieran had stepped out onto the two-lane road, hoping to spot another vehicle or a house close by. He couldn't see anything even with his enhanced sight.

He'd pulled the jacket closer around himself and settled in to wait. If no one came in an hour, he'd have to hoof it to the nearest town. He had plenty of money, the only thing his father had given him when he'd sent him away, so getting another vehicle shouldn't be too hard.

It had only been twenty minutes before he'd spotted headlights headed his way. When the driver pulled over to the side and stepped out, Kieran had smiled. A shifter. They would surely help another paranormal. Kieran had been raised in a small town up in the mountains and had only known other Walkers like his family and humans. Very seldom did a shifter come around, but there had been a few occasions one would stop by to speak with his father. Caspar had enjoyed learning about other cultures.

He walked forward with his hand out.

Out of nowhere he'd been struck on the back of his head. As he'd fallen to his knees, he'd heard laughing. Right before at least three people began to beat him.

At eighteen and away from his family for the first time, he had been terrified when he'd woken in the cage, alone, naked and in pain.

Now Kieran wasn't even sure how long he'd been held by that point. It seemed like a lifetime had passed already.

Sometimes he hadn't seen anyone for what had to be days and he would wonder if they'd forgotten about him and left him to starve. Other times the days ran together as his enemies spent their time torturing and abusing him.

He'd prayed for his suffering to end. For all of it to end.

Kieran gasped as he came out of the memory and found himself at his desk. He was trembling, chilled to the bone, and the video had stopped playing. He jumped to his feet to stalk over to the liquor bar.

He poured two fingers of whiskey before tossing it back then refilling the glass. The alcohol did nothing to warm him, but hopefully it would help settle his nerves.

"Damn," he muttered, strolling to the large windows behind his desk. He yanked open the curtains, not even thinking about the noise he'd make. Too distraught to remember Dakota, until he heard the bed shift.

He froze, hoping she hadn't woken. He didn't want her to see him like this. When her breathing evened back out, Kieran sighed in relief and peered out of the window.

The bright lights of the Strip twinkled below him. Even now, at three o'clock in the morning, there would be people running around, walking, some drunk, some just high on life.

They were alive and unaware real monsters watched them from the dark. One wrong move, one misstep and they could become someone's victim. Just like he'd been.

He leaned forward and rested his forehead against the cool glass. The feeling of helplessness gnawed at him until the first tear fell down his cheek.

Chapter Three

Kieran decided to order room service instead of using the kitchen in the suite. He didn't like to cook and the restaurant in the hotel was amazing. He placed his order for three along with two large pots of coffee before he hung up and strolled to the bedroom.

He pushed open the door and stared.

Even though it was still chilly to him in the room, Dakota had kicked off the covers and was lying naked on her side of the bed. The way her fingers stretched out toward his side made his heart flutter. Was she reaching for him? Even in her sleep?

Kieran sauntered to the bed and ran his fingers through her long hair. She'd had it trimmed and the color re-done recently and he loved it. Her light brown hair had a mixture of blond, darker brown and red highlights that seemed to match her personality perfectly. She was a serious agent, but there were so many layers to her. Dakota could be fun and free while also strong and independent. Like the colors in her hair, she wasn't just one thing. Every day when he looked at her, he was amazed.

"Hmm," Dakota murmured as she stretched. She blinked her eyes opened before smiling at him. "Hi."

"Morning," he greeted. He bent and gave her a quick kiss then pulled back.

She caught his sweater in her hand. "Why are you dressed?"

It was weird for him not to greet her naked and wanting in the morning. There was nothing better than starting off his day with a reminder she belonged to him. "Jackson is coming for breakfast. I let you sleep in as much as possible, but he'll be here in about fifteen minutes."

She groaned before releasing him. As she sat up, her gaze went to the alarm clock next to the bed. "It's five-forty in the morning?"

"Yeah," he told her.

"We've only been asleep for four hours?"

"I know, but I thought you might want to join us?" He could have let her sleep. Since they both worked the late shift, that was when most of their work needed to be done and they normally didn't get out of bed until late morning or almost noon.

"You'd better have ordered coffee," she declared before dragging herself off the mattress.

"I did." He knew his lover.

She grunted as she headed into the bathroom. He would make it up to her. Dakota was not a morning person on the best of days and he knew if it wasn't Jackson, who she was trying to be friends with, she would have rolled over and ignored him.

He heard the shower turn on but since he couldn't join her this time, he strode back out into the main area of the suite.

The luxury suite had two bedrooms with a large living area, dining room and kitchen, plus a big open-plan office. The room smelled of Dakota and he never got tired of the scent.

Kieran was so used to using his extra senses he didn't really notice when he was. It had become as natural as breathing. Humans picked up aromas from the items and environment they were in. Shifters did as well, but also had the aroma of their animal nature. Walkers, however, never gave off any scent. They didn't pick up any or leave any behind.

So others wouldn't be able to tell he'd been in the room for almost a month. But Dakota—her sweet and sexy scent had mixed with everything he owned. When he went to work, he smelt her on his clothes. He wished he could have her fragrance mixed with his on his skin.

"So why are we doing this at six in the morning?"

Kieran jumped, not having heard Dakota finish her shower or dress. She strolled into the room, drying her hair with a towel. She wore a faded pair of jeans and a white T-shirt. Her feet were bare, with the nails painted light pink. Fuck, he'd never had a foot fetish before, but he actually wanted to suck on her toes. What the hell was wrong with him? She would probably laugh at him if he shared his latest thought.

"Hey! You okay?" she asked as she approached.

He couldn't admit he was almost dead on his feet, that the nights of not sleeping were starting to take their toll. "Yeah, lost in thought."

"That's been happening a lot lately." She tossed the towel onto the couch before she reached out to cup his face. "I've been waiting for you to talk to me about what's going on."

Guilt flooded him. Still, she already put up with a lot from him. "I'm just trying to come to terms with everything. Caspar being gone, my transfer here and seeing Jackson."

"I know." She rose to the tips of her toes and kissed him lightly. "It seems like so much longer than a month when I think of everything that's happened. But, on the other hand, it doesn't seem like I've had that long with you yet."

He wrapped his arm around her waist and tugged her closer. "I know what you mean." He brushed his lips over hers before pressing harder and licking her.

A knock interrupted them. He didn't even have to breathe deeply to know it was their food. The strong aroma of coffee drifted to him.

"I'll get it," he told her before giving her one more peck.

Kieran walked to the door. Dakota grabbed the towel then headed back toward the bedroom. He unlocked then opened the door to the room service attendant.

"Good morning, sir." The young man greeted him with his hand on the rolling trolley.

"Morning. You can bring it in and set up at the table." He

couldn't remember the guy's name, although he'd dropped off food several times now.

"Yes, sir." The guy stepped past him, pushing the cart.

Kieran heard the elevator ding and glanced into the hall. He spotted Jackson exiting and grinned at his friend.

When they'd been in the hellhole of Mount Fauna, Jackson hadn't weighed more than a hundred and thirty pounds. Now his friend had bulked up and the way he carried himself screamed power and money.

Each time Kieran saw Jackson, it was still hard to believe Jackson hadn't been killed like Kieran had once thought. His friend had been dumped and left for dead, but found even before Kieran had been.

"Hey," Jackson said as he looked at Kieran with tired eyes.

Concern had Kieran reaching out and pulling Jackson close as soon as he was within distance. "Are you okay?"

Jackson shook his head. "Thanks for getting up early for this. I know you both work late."

"It's fine," Kieran assured him. "Come on."

Kieran turned and almost smacked into the waiter he'd forgotten about. The young man danced out of the way.

"Sorry, sir," he apologized to Kieran.

"My fault." Kieran reached for the black envelope that would require his signature. He made sure to give the guy a good-sized tip before signing his name and handing it back.

"Have a good morning, sir." He nodded to Kieran.

"You too," Kieran replied. He glanced behind him and saw Jackson had his back turned to his employee. That was strange.

Once the young man had gone, Kieran closed and locked the door. "What's going on?"

Jackson took a deep breath. "Is Dakota joining us? I think it would be better to tell you both at once."

"I'm right here," Dakota said as she exited the bedroom. She'd brushed her hair, but it was still wet and she remained barefoot. "Let's get some coffee. You look like you could use it."

"Please," Jackson replied. He gripped Kieran's hand and gave him a quick, hard squeeze before going to join Dakota.

She was already pouring coffee into three mugs at the table. Jackson accepted his with quiet thanks. Kieran hurried toward them just in time for her to hand him his.

"Let's sit and talk."

"What's wrong?" Kieran pressed.

Jackson took a sip of the hot drink before he sighed. "Alex has disappeared. I've searched all night for him and there's no sign of him anywhere."

Dakota shook her head. "Tell us everything."

Jackson's hand was trembling, so Kieran gripped his wrist to try to settle his friend. Alex was Jackson's number two man and from what he'd learned, Alex had been at Jackson's side since he'd returned from Mount Fauna. They'd grown up together and the entire time Jackson had been missing, his best friend had never stopped searching.

"There was a rumor of a couple of Walkers coming to town," Jackson said.

Kieran knew from what Jackson had told him before that he monitored all paranormals who came into his city. He owned more hotels, casinos and restaurants in the area than any other single person. He had been part of bringing Vegas back to being the top travel destination. In the early two thousands, the city had grown dirty and run-down. But Jackson had helped get the tourists to return.

Part of that was making sure the city stayed safe for the visitors. He had an entire network of employees who watched vehicles, buses, planes and everything else for anyone who might want to cause trouble for innocents. It was no surprise Alex would research the appearance of Walkers.

"He left here around nine last night. The two Walkers had been spotted hitting some of the casinos farther up the Strip. I don't know if they were avoiding my places, or just hadn't made it around here yet."

"Do you have any of the information Alex was using?" Dakota asked.

Jackson nodded. "Not all of it was acquired by legal means, but I have everything he had."

"Don't worry about that." Dakota waved her hand. "We're not known for always following legal lines. Some of us less than others." She glanced over at him and Kieran grinned back. He did have a tendency of not caring about rules. So what?

"You'll help me?" Jackson asked quietly.

Kieran was still grasping his wrist and Dakota reached over and laid her hand over his. "We will find him."

Jackson dropped his head to the table and Kieran stood so he could comfort him. He pressed his hand against his friend's neck. It was hard to see Jackson breaking when they'd both worked so hard to get their lives back on track.

Once Jackson was breathing more easily, he nodded and Kieran retook his seat.

"I've been up all night. I knew something was wrong right away. He called me from his phone before eleven, but no one was there. I could hear a scuffle but couldn't pick up much of what was going on. I sent some of my guys out immediately and we found his cell in an alley."

"Do you have it with you?" Dakota asked.

Jackson pulled it from his pocket and slid it over the table to her.

"We'll figure this out. I'm going to make some calls. I know you don't want to eat, but I need you to," she said to Jackson before glancing at Kieran. "We have to keep his strength up."

"Yeah," Kieran agreed. He waited until Dakota had stood and strolled away from them, heading toward the bedroom, before he turned his attention back to Jackson. "She's right. You need to eat. You've been up all night, but we're not going to rest until we bring Alex home."

"He never stopped looking for me," Jackson whispered.

"I know. And we'll find him soon."

Jackson breathed deeply. "I already have my guys out there looking. They haven't heard anything about Alex, but there's talk about some shifters that have gone missing."

"Yes," Kieran said. "Four we know about so far. I think there's more that haven't been reported. I don't really know how many total."

"No Walkers?"

Kieran was with Jackson on where his thoughts were going. "Not that we know about."

"Is this really happening? Could he have been taken with the shifters?"

"I don't know," Kieran admitted.

"He won't be able to handle it," Jackson muttered. "If it's shifters doing this or even if he's locked up with shifters. It will kill him."

Dakota was coming back quietly into the room, but Kieran didn't take his eyes off Jackson.

"I knew something had to have happened to him with how he reacted to Remy. He always seemed okay with Dakota, though," Kieran mused.

"He didn't blame all the shifters," Jackson explained. "He was actually always trying to get me past my own prejudice. But it's still hard to for him to be anywhere near a wolf shifter."

Dakota didn't interrupt but began to load up plates with the food Kieran had ordered earlier. Jackson continued talking even as she set a pile of eggs, bacon, sausage, biscuits and gravy, and some fruit near him.

She placed his hand on his fork and Jackson ate as he spoke.

"He fell in love with a sweet wolf shifter named Tina," Jackson continued. "Her parents wanted her to marry another wolf shifter from their Pack and forbade her from seeing him. They were sixteen when they first started dating. They hid it for a few years, but as soon as they were eighteen, she told her parents she was going to be with

Alex."

Kieran found a plate in front of him as well and since the food was there, he ate.

"She moved out of the territory and into a house with Alex and his parents. The entire Pack harassed them, but Alex wouldn't let her go back. Nine months after she moved in, Tina's parents, brother, Alpha and a few enforcers burnt the house down and when Alex, Tina and his parents escaped, they beat them so badly Alex was the only survivor."

"Fuck." Kieran regretted even the few bites of breakfast he'd taken.

"He was in a coma for three months before he woke. Our family were old friends and even though it took another two months before he was released from the hospital, I spent every day with him. He came home with me and I helped him heal. Until the day I was taken."

Kieran had to look away from his friend. His gaze caught on Dakota and she had tears pooled in her eyes. She cared so much about other people. He knew she would have done everything she could to find Alex even if she hadn't heard the story. But now she knew what he'd suffered, she would push even harder.

"We have to find him," Jackson finished.

"I'm dropping Alex's phone off to my old partner," Dakota said. "You've worked with him before and he'll keep any secrets he comes across, but he's the best."

"I always trusted Dean." Jackson nodded.

"My current partners, Gabe and Dare, will be here in less than an hour. They need to see the footage of Alex leaving. You don't have to show them anything that took place in your office. But they'll start there and retrace his steps. I know you have your own men working on this also. Keep them out there. The more help we have, the better."

Jackson looked relieved. "I was worried you'd want me to keep my people out of your way."

"No." Dakota shook her head. "Your Walkers might be able to get more out of people. I heard you ask about the missing shifters…"

"Yes. I wonder if the same people are responsible," Jackson said.

"Me too," she replied. "And if they've moved to taking Walkers, they've either grown bold or aren't scared. Anyone who knows you, knows Alex. If they knew who Alex was, then they will expect you to look. We want to make sure your guys are visible."

"That makes sense," Jackson agreed.

"What if this is a ploy to draw you out?" Kieran voiced his concern.

"I've thought about that too," Dakota said. "We'll use your resources. Anything you have, but you can't leave the hotel."

Jackson stiffened. "I have to look for him."

"No," Dakota argued. "You have to stay safe so you don't end up with Alex."

"If that will lead us to him—"

"Give us time," Dakota urged. "I'm not saying you'll be a prisoner, but give us a chance to find him before you go offering yourself as a sacrifice."

Jackson glanced at him and Kieran nodded.

"Fine," Jackson agreed. "I'll work from here and coordinate the teams. But you have to keep me informed."

"I promise," Kieran assured him.

"Okay." Jackson ran his hand roughly over his face. "Where do we start?"

* * * *

Kieran hadn't been in the lab where Dean worked. The two of them hadn't started off on the best foot after Caspar had asked his nephew, Dean, to spy on Kieran when Kieran had first gotten to town. Kieran didn't like anyone in his business and liked even less that he hadn't spotted the human. It still pissed him off that Dean had managed to follow him for several days before Kieran had known.

Plus, Kieran didn't even find out by catching him. No — Dean had told him after Kieran had stopped three shifters from attacking two humans in an alley. He'd taken care of the shifters but then called in to the local Organization for them to pick up the men. That was also the same night Kieran had met Dakota. So while not everything that night had been bad, Kieran still held a grudge against and a small amount of respect for Dean.

Dean sat at a desk with three monitors scrolling while he typed furiously. It was obvious Dakota was comfortable in Dean's work space as she strolled right in and hopped up on one of the tables. Kieran walked in more slowly before settling against the wall and leaning with his arms crossed over his chest. Dean didn't even look up at them when they entered.

He barely held back a growl until Dakota peered over at him and shook her head. Kieran grumbled under his breath until Dean looked up and turned in Kieran's direction.

"Oh!" Dean said, blushing. "I didn't hear you come in."

"Obviously," Kieran muttered.

Dakota glared at him before she jumped off the table and walked over to Dean. "Whatcha working on?"

"I have this computer running all the known victims for any connections we might have missed. If they shopped at the same grocery store, if they went to the same doctor, if they used the same bank — everything. If we just find one link, we might know how and who they're targeting," Dean explained.

"Sound good," Dakota said.

"This one" — Dean pointed to another screen — "is screening every crime in the city that could have been perpetrated by a paranormal. And, finally, the last one is looking for places that the shifters could be held. Recent rentals, leases or purchases. We're checking every name and corporation. They have to have somewhere they're taking the shifters to." Dean looked over his shoulder at Kieran. "I added as much as I could, including your friend.

There some variables I want to play with, but I need more information about him."

Kieran nodded as Dakota pulled a card out of her pocket. "This is Jackson's IT guy. You two can work together and compare notes."

"Cool." Dean took the card and stuck it in his keyboard. "Now," he said as he rolled his chair away from the desk to another work station. "I hacked into the city traffic cameras."

"You what?" Kieran asked, surprised. "*Hacked?*"

Dean laughed. "I can admit I'm really enjoying my new job."

Kieran couldn't help but smile. Maybe he was starting to like Dean just a little bit.

"Anyway, I think I found something."

"What?" Kieran pushed off the wall and stalked forward as Dean started typing something in.

"I already sent this to Gabe and Dare. They were checking on another tip and were close to the area." Dean stood and pointed to the screen. "Watch this."

The video was a common feed Kieran had seen before during other investigations. Most of the cities used the same programs.

"That's Alex's car." Dean pointed at the black BMW on the screen. "I can't get a good view from this angle, but I'm sure it's him. He pulled into the alley, keeping us from seeing where he's going but…" Dean punched some buttons that had the image fast-forwarding. "Thirty-seven minutes later."

The interior of the vehicle was visible. It was fucking visible. Kieran peered closer. "That's not Alex."

"No, but…" Dean did something that zoomed in. "Look in the back seat."

There he was. Alex was in the back behind the passenger seat. His head was tipped back and Kieran doubted the man had been awake. There was another person next to him.

"Can you clean that up?" Kieran demanded.

"Trying," Dean said. "The good news is Alex has OnStar. We're tracking him. Or Gabe and Dare are."

"What?" Kieran yelled. "Why didn't you tell me that earlier?"

"Because I'm having trouble staying connected. I could give Gabe and Dare general directions but, until either a warrant comes through or I figure out how to get past the last firewall, I'm only getting bits and pieces."

"Well, fix it!" Kieran shouted.

"Hey." Dakota grabbed Kieran's face. "Calm down. Dean will figure this out. But in the meantime, we have a solid lead. We need to get hold of Jackson and update him. Then we'll head out ourselves."

Kieran wanted… He didn't know what the hell he wanted. Dean had done more in a couple of hours than Kieran could have managed. The guy really did make a good lab rat.

He pulled away from Dakota and stomped to Dean. Dean stood, just staring back at him. Kieran had to swallow several times, then he looked Dean in the eye. "Thank you."

Dean nodded. "We'll find him. We'll find them all. Maybe Jackson's guy will be able to help get me past the firewall. While he's doing that, I'll work on cleaning up the video of Alex's car. I'll send it to you as soon as I have something."

There wasn't anything left to say, so Kieran backed up and pulled his cell out of his pocket. At least he had some news to share with Jackson. He rushed from the room even as he pressed the number.

* * * *

Alex Hamilton groaned from the pounding in his head. He didn't remember drinking the night before, so there was no way he should feel so damn shitty. He was also very fucking uncomfortable. Freezing, since he was naked.

He tried to roll over but found it more difficult than he'd expected. His body heavy and his limbs not cooperating. Very slowly, he blinked his eyes open. He was lying on his back and above him all he could see were metal bars. He frowned, blinked some more, then turned his head. More bars were on the side. He was in a cage.

"Fuck," he muttered as he slowly sat up.

"Hey, man, you okay?"

Alex turned toward the voice and it took all his control not to flinch. The naked man in the cell beside him was a wolf shifter. Fuck, that couldn't be good. He wouldn't have partied with a wolf the night before. And he had a really bad feeling he wasn't in a city jail.

Alex squinted to get a better look at the young man. He was shocked by his appearance. He actually had to lift his hand and place it over his mouth, trying to hold in bile when he got a good look at the condition of the wolf. The guy was covered in dirt and filth, but the obvious signs of torture turned Alex's stomach.

"Who did this to you?" Alex demanded.

The wolf shifter was pretty young and it appeared he'd been thoroughly beaten. He also had thin cuts across his stomach.

"I have no idea," the kid said. "I woke up just like you did. I can't remember what day that was. It seems like years ago. Some men, shifters, come and take me to another room. That's when they do this." He waved his hand over his body.

"No!" Horror filled Alex. He'd seen similar wounds like that before. Frantically, he began to search around the room, but all he could see was more cages. Some were filled, but several remained empty. This couldn't be happening. There was no way Alex had been captured by the same monsters who'd taken Jackson and Kieran earlier.

"I would say it's going to be okay, but I'm pretty sure we're screwed," the wolf shifter said.

Alex shook his head. The shifter had no idea how bad it was going to get. "What's your name?" He really didn't want to be friendly with the guy, but the circumstances were dire and he might need an ally or two. Even if he had to depend on a fucking wolf.

"Max."

Alex scooted closer to the side where Max leaned against his own bars. "Here's the thing, Max," Alex said. "I'm pretty sure I know the group that took us."

"What do they want?" Max asked. "I tried to talk to them, but all they did was put a gag in my mouth and torture me."

"Yeah, that's pretty much how they work."

"What do we do?"

"Try to stay alive," Alex murmured. "My boss is a very powerful man. He'll already be looking for me. If we can just hang on, he'll rescue us."

"I was hoping my Alpha would be able to find me," Max said as he dropped his head.

"I'm sure he's trying." Alex tried to give comfort. He didn't know anything about the Alpha. Jackson gave over anything that had to do with the wolves to one of the other guys. "I never heard of this group taking shifters, though, so this is new."

"I don't know how long some of them have been here." Max pointed farther down the aisle. "But I think one of the guys might be dead."

"Shit." Alex closed his eyes. Because of his connection with Jackson and Kieran, he knew the Organization was currently looking for the people who now held him. That made them very lucky. In the years Jackson and Kieran had been missing, no one knew who was responsible. "Don't fight them. Do whatever they tell you. Escape will be almost impossible, but we will be rescued."

"You sound sure," Max whispered.

He had to be. If Alex let himself think about what was going to be done to him, he wouldn't last a day. "I am."

Max groaned and grabbed his stomach. "I'm so hungry."

Yeah, Alex was aware the monsters loved to starve their prisoners. Jackson had been so malnourished that, even with his Walker genes, it had taken months to get rid of his sunken skin and gain just a little weight. "I know."

"I don't know why they took me. It's not like I'm anyone in my Pack. I thought it was because of an article I was working on, but now I don't think so."

"I doubt that's the reason," Alex agreed. "You were either in the wrong place at the wrong time, or they targeted you because you're a shifter."

"Which do you think it is?"

"I don't think it matters." If Bradley was responsible for their current circumstances, then nothing would matter but staying alive. Even if Alex was surrounded by shifters.

A loud bang on the opposite side of the room had Alex jerking his head in that direction. The other prisoners scrambled, lurched and crawled as far away from the fronts of their cages as possible.

Two men strolled in and they were both smiling. Alex clenched his fists. It might take time, but eventually he was going to knock those smug looks off their faces.

As they sauntered down the aisle, they hit cages, bared fangs and laughed. Oh yeah, these two were first-grade assholes.

"Looky here," the big muscular mountain of a man said, stopping in front of Alex. "Our first Walker."

Alex didn't respond.

The smaller blond stepped beside the mountain man. "I don't know, Bruce," he said. "He doesn't look so dangerous."

Bruce threw back his head and laughed. "Don't let the boss hear you say that, Craig. He's got a hard-on for these Walkers."

Craig merely shrugged before sneering at Alex. "Whatever."

It was hard to keep his head down and just take in all the scents of the two guards. Bruce was a grizzly bear shifter and it smelt like he hadn't showered in days. The stench was almost overpowering. Craig, a cheetah shifter, appeared to take better care of himself, but the strong odor of stale cigarettes wafted from him. If these were the best two this group had, Alex knew Jackson, Kieran and the Organization were going to rip them apart.

He didn't even try to hide the smile on his face.

"What do you think you're smiling at?" Craig asked him.

Alex remained silent.

"He won't be smiling soon," Bruce said as he punched four numbers into a keypad next to Alex's cage door. It was too quick for Alex's tired mind to catch, but a couple more times and he would get the code.

The door clinked then released. Bruce stepped in first with Craig right at his back. Alex attempted to move, but his body wasn't under his control. Bruce grinned as he stalked forward and grabbed him by the neck. Bruce lifted him and Alex could only grunt as he was hanging in the man's hold.

"You got a pretty face now," Bruce taunted. "But we're gonna change that."

Alex did the only thing he could. He spit in Bruce's face.

Craig cackled as he reared back his fist.

Fuck, that was going to hurt.

Chapter Four

As the city disappeared in the rear-view mirror, Dakota worked as best she could on her phone. Email, text messages and phone calls were coming in fast, leaving a lot of information to get through. Kieran drove with precision and speed as he spoke to Jackson on his Bluetooth.

Dakota tuned out Kieran's conversation as she looked at the map Dean had sent her. He'd marked out possible locations in the Red Rock area. It made sense that whoever had taken Alex and the shifters would set up base out in the expansive mountains outside Las Vegas. Much like Mount Fauna, the Red Rocks were isolated with numerous caves and caverns.

Gabe and Dare were already there, waiting on them with Jackson and Remy on their way as well. The plan was to meet up before they broke off in teams and began their search.

Her phone dinged and she saw a message from her boss.

We got company. The Coalition.

"Shit!" she muttered.

"What?" Kieran asked, making her jump.

She hadn't realized Kieran had disconnected from Jackson. She glanced over at him, trying to decide what to say. The Shifter Coalition had been formed several years ago when the shifters around the globe had gone public. There'd been a lot of panic from humans who had thought the shifters were trying to take over the world. The Coalition was a government agency run by shifters to police other shifters and also protect them from danger and prejudice.

"Just tell me," Kieran said.

"Sparro just texted. The Coalition is at the office."

"Fuck! Fuck! Fuck!" Kieran banged his fist on the steering wheel before jerking it to the side and slamming his foot on the brake. He pushed open the door and was out before Dakota had even processed they'd stopped.

This was going to be worse than she'd thought.

Stall as long as you can. We are chasing down a lead.

She sent the two sentences to Sparro before putting her phone back in her pocket. Kieran was pacing in front of the SUV, but it didn't seem to be doing anything to calm him. Instead, he was growing more agitated.

Dakota quietly exited the vehicle and waited on the side of the road until Kieran looked at her. It broke her heart to see the fear on his face.

"K," she whispered.

"I can't do it," he said in a rough voice. "I can't work with them."

"I know," she assured him. It pushed Kieran's boundaries to have him at the office as it was. There were very few Walkers and under his old boss Kieran hadn't been required to make appearances often. The shifter Coalition worked with them in investigations fairly often, but Kieran had never been part of those teams. There was a limit on how many shifters Kieran could stand to be around.

"This was never supposed to happen," he said, striding forward. He gripped her arms and hauled her closer. "I'm supposed to be in the shadows. No one knew about me, cared, or needed anything from me. I don't know how to handle this!"

She needed to calm him down. It worried her that he was freaking out. Kieran was so strong and steady when it came to work. He knew what had to be done and had no issues following through. They were going to need him in top form to find Alex and the missing shifters. "It's going to be okay," she told him. "You're not alone. You'll never be alone again."

Kieran snorted. "I think that's my point."

Dakota found herself relaxing when Kieran was able to joke. Her lover tried so hard to show her only control — she knew it was tearing him apart to be vulnerable where she could see. He thought she didn't know he hadn't been sleeping lately, but Dakota was more tuned in to him than he knew.

Not only was there attraction and strong feelings between them, but her jaguar had accepted Kieran as well. She might not have claimed him, marked him with her teeth, but Kieran was hers. He would have to come to terms with her animal eventually, but she could wait on that. However, sooner rather than later, Kieran needed to realize she wanted every part of him — the good and the bad.

"I won't let anything happen to you," Dakota told him.

"What?" he jerked back. "You think I'm worried about myself?"

Confused, Dakota nodded slightly.

"No." He yanked her close once again. "It's so much worse."

"I don't understand," she confessed.

Kieran sighed before brushing a kiss on her temple. He stepped back and turned. She didn't move. If whatever he had to say was done easier not looking at her, she would deal with it.

"If it was just me in danger, I could run," Kieran said. "I have enough money, training and contacts that if I disappeared, no one would ever be able to find me."

She shivered at the coldness in his tone. How often had he contemplated just that?

"They already took Alex," he said. "What if they get Jackson again, or Remy? What if Caspar gets caught up in this? He's human — he wouldn't last a day of their torture."

She knew he was right.

"What if—?" He began to breathe roughly. He spun around and his eyes were glowing. "What if they got their hands on you?"

Oh, God, she wished she knew the right words to say and take away his fear. Because that was what he was afraid of most. Losing those around him he had begun to care about.

"What if," she said quietly, "because of the bonds you've made with all of us, we're able to stop them this time? For good."

Kieran shook his head. "It's too risky."

"No. If you hadn't connected with Caspar, then Remy and finally me, we wouldn't be as strong as we are now."

"They can't get any of you," Kieran said. "They can't."

"They can't get you either," she replied.

Kieran nodded. "I still can't work with the Coalition. I know I promised I wouldn't ignore your jaguar and I really am working on it. But I can't be around those other shifters."

"You don't have to," she told him. "Trust me."

His eyes had gone back to normal and the tension lines on his face had eased. "I do trust you."

The confession was heartfelt and all she needed to hear. She could ignore the reminder he still hadn't accepted her jaguar.

"Then let's meet with the others and find Alex." She held out her hand. He took it before lifting her wrist to his lips and running his tongue over her pulse.

"Later," he said when she reached for him.

"Ass," she told him fondly.

"Yes, and I have a spectacular one," he teased.

He did, but if she started to think about that, they would never get to the meeting. "Let's go."

Dakota returned to the SUV, ignoring Kieran's chuckle. The crisis had passed for the moment, but she knew it wasn't over. Kieran and Jackson were both going to have to deal with the ghosts of the past. Whatever was happening to Alex as they searched was going to be difficult for both the Walkers to handle.

"We should be almost there," Kieran said as they settled back in their seats.

Dakota pulled out her phone and clicked on the map again. "Five more miles, then we'll take the first turn-off. Gabe and Dare should already be there."

"We can't stop until we find Alex," Kieran replied, putting the car in drive. "I can't let him suffer the way I did."

"I know." Dakota slid her palm over his thigh. "We won't."

* * * *

Kieran peered around at the ragtag group that had gathered to begin the search. He and Dakota had met up with Gabe and Dare right before Remy had pulled up. Jackson had followed with four of his own men, all Walkers.

Now the ten of them were dividing the rocky cliffs of the Red Rocks into search zones.

"One Walker with each shifter or human," Jackson said.

Kieran glanced at Gabe, the only human.

"What?" he asked with a snarl. "I can take care of myself."

"He's probably the safest one here," Remy said. "They don't have much use for a human."

Kieran snorted. "That we know of. They didn't take shifters last time either. There's no point to it. Bradley is an eagle shifter. What does he need from other shifters?"

"That's a good question," Jackson said.

"Maybe this isn't Bradley," Dare suggested.

"It is," Kieran and Jackson said at the same time. It was something Kieran felt deep down. What was happening with the shifters, Alex's disappearance, Caspar getting a lead that took him away from Kieran's side and leading Kieran to the city, all went back to the time Bradley had held him and Jackson.

"So what is this?" Jackson asked. "Revenge?"

"Then why take the shifters?" Remy questioned. "If we didn't know about the shifters, we might not have moved so fast on Alex going missing."

"I would have known something was wrong," Jackson said.

"But would you have gone to Kieran in just hours?" Remy asked.

"Probably not," Jackson admitted.

"Exactly," Remy said. "So why tip us off? They have to need something from the shifters."

"So again," Dare said, "how can we be sure it's Bradley?"

Kieran clenched his teeth to keep from biting Dare's head off. Dare didn't understand what he and Jackson had been through. He couldn't comprehend the effect years of torture had on someone. Deep in his gut, Kieran knew Bradley was involved.

"It doesn't matter," Dakota said. "We need to find Alex and the shifters."

"Then maybe you should have asked the Alpha of this territory for help," a new voice said behind them.

Kieran spun and crouched at the unknown threat. As he moved, Jackson leapt to his side and ended up in the same position.

"Shit," Remy muttered.

"Calm down." The stranger raised his hands. "I came to help."

"Help?" Kieran snapped. He didn't know what this wolf shifter Alpha asshole was doing there, but it was pretty suspicious. "How did you know where we were?"

"I had him followed," the stranger replied, motioning to Remy.

"Followed?" Remy asked. "Really?"

"Do you blame me?" the Alpha asked.

Kieran did not like his partner's integrity being questioned. He straightened to his full height and glowered at the Alpha.

"No." Remy shook his head before glancing over at Kieran. "It's okay, K. I really should have suspected it."

"That doesn't mean he's welcome," Jackson said as he

stalked toward their unwanted guest. "You weren't invited here, wolf."

"Calm down, Walker," the Alpha said. "I am only here to help."

Dakota stepped forward and in front of Kieran and Jackson. Kieran started to grab her to yank her back. He didn't want Dakota anywhere near a wolf shifter he didn't know. Remy neatly stepped in his way so Kieran's hand fell on his shoulder instead.

"Just wait," Remy whispered.

Kieran didn't know why he bothered whispering, since everyone except the one human would still be able to hear.

"I'm Dakota, with the Organization," she said to the Alpha. "I understand why you might have trouble believing we're doing everything we can to find your missing Pack mates, but Remy and all of us are trying."

"Alpha Damon Fincher, but you can call me Damon," the Alpha said. "I've heard about you, Dakota Reese, as well as everyone here. I do see your Organization is working on the case, but I also think we all know there is more to this than just some kidnappings."

Dakota glanced over her shoulder and he could see the question in his eyes. How the hell were they going to get rid of the Alpha?

"We don't have time for this," Kieran said, stepping forward, shoulder to shoulder with Dakota. "Leave us so we can try to find your people."

"Or I can help," Damon told him. "I know this area better than anyone else."

"Then point on the map where we should be searching," Jackson ordered.

Damon crossed his arms over his chest. "I've done my homework on you, Walker. The man who decided to keep watch over an entire city of transients. Very ambitious."

"I didn't ask for your approval," Jackson replied.

Kieran really didn't like standing in between the two dominant paranormal creatures and liked the fact that

Dakota was also in the middle. He still didn't know a lot of his friend's past or how he'd ended up in Vegas, but he trusted Jackson. He couldn't say the same for the Alpha wolf.

He wasn't surprised when Damon's gaze landed on him. "Kieran Smith, you're a legend. I didn't think you actually existed."

"Well, now you can see I do," Kieran replied.

"You've killed members of my Pack," Damon claimed.

Kieran couldn't be certain whether he had or not. He'd taken out a lot of shifters after he joined the Organization. When he'd first become an agent, it was just cleaner and easier to kill the paranormal creatures who'd attacked innocents.

"Are you threatening him?" Remy's words ended with a growl.

"No," Damon said. "They were killed because they broke the rules. In a Pack as large as mine, I've had to become accustomed to losing some of my members."

"You don't seem too upset," Kieran accused.

"Nothing I can do about the ones that break the law. I've had to put a few down myself," Damon said. "It's the innocents I won't allow harm to come to. My two missing? They don't deserve whatever is happening to them right now."

That was about the only thing Kieran would ever agree with the Alpha about. No one deserved what Bradley did to those he captured.

"Now, if you're done wasting time," Damon said, "let's start hunting." He strolled over to where Gabe and Dare had spread out a large map on the hood of their car.

"We don't need your help," Jackson told him.

"Doesn't matter," Damon replied. "I'm going whether you want me to or not. If we team up, we'll get more ground covered."

Kieran walked to Jackson's side and leaned in. "Whatever you want to do, I'll back you." He meant his promise too.

Jackson wasn't any fonder of shifters than Kieran was.

"Damn," Jackson murmured. "We're wasting time."

"Fine," Kieran said. "We'll let him tag along, but we keep an eye on him. He could be leading us straight into a trap."

"I can hear you," Damon sing-songed, still bent over the map.

"I already hate him," Kieran said loudly.

Damon snorted in response.

"Come look at this, Walkers." Damon waved them over.

They all moved and Kieran was pleased when Jackson put himself on the other side of Dakota. Anyone would have to get through both him and Jackson to hurt her.

"You can rule out this section." He took the marker out of Gabe's pocket and circled an area. "That's where my Pack runs. We would have smelt any other shifter near."

Kieran exchanged a look with Jackson. That was pretty convenient. Suspicious. Jackson gave him a nod. Jackson agreed.

"I'll allow you to search there later if you still don't trust me or we don't find them. But we need to concentrate on these areas." Again, Damon circled four different areas.

Kieran glanced at the Alpha, surprised by his offer.

"I'm not your enemy," Damon told him.

"You're not my friend either."

"Maybe not," Damon replied. "But if we can rescue everyone that has been taken, the point will be moot."

"We have a starting point," Remy said. "We should get going."

"Who's the Alpha going with?" Dare asked.

"Me," Kieran answered right away. He wasn't going to let anyone else run the risk of the Alpha turning on them.

"I'm with you too," Dakota said.

"I'll take Jackson with me," Remy threw in.

"We'll split up my guys with the human and bear," Jackson added.

Kieran really wanted to argue about having Dakota close to the Alpha, but when he looked at her, she was preparing for his argument.

"Fine," he agreed.

Dakota appeared shocked but quickly schooled her features. "Let's go then."

"One more thing," Damon said. "It would be better if those of us who can, shifted. We'll move faster and our senses will be stronger."

"No!" Remy and Dakota said in unison.

Kieran closed his eyes. The Alpha had a point. The shifters would be able to move faster and better in their animal form. He just didn't know if he could handle being around so many in their other forms. When he was hunting or working and came across his prey in their animal forms, he had no problem because he planned on taking them out. While he wasn't comfortable with Remy's wolf, he didn't freak and attack him either. But he didn't know how he would react to Dakota. What if he had a bad reaction to her jaguar and she finally realized how much better she could do than him?

Damn it, life had been so much simpler when he didn't care what other people thought of him.

"Hey," Dakota said as she slipped her hand in his. "It's okay. We'll stay human."

"No," Kieran said before he even had time to think about what he was saying. "We knew I'd have to meet your jaguar eventually."

"Not like this," she said quietly.

"Uh," Remy said loudly. "Let's give them a minute."

Kieran was glad Remy understood and shuffled the others away. He turned to Dakota and cupped her face. "You need to do this."

"I don't want to lose you."

"You won't," he assured her. "I may be an asshole most of the time, but even I know you're the best thing that ever happened to me. It's time I accepted every part of you."

She stared into his eyes as though she was looking for any deceit in his words. Kieran simply looked right back at her.

"You're sure?"

"Yes," he told her. "Yes."

Dakota rose to her tiptoes and kissed him deeply. He wrapped his arms around her and let her ravage his mouth. All he could do now was pray this wasn't the last time he tasted her.

She pulled back slowly. "Okay."

It was the hardest thing she'd ever done. Dakota strolled away from Kieran to prepare for her shift. All of the times she had pictured sharing her jaguar with Kieran and the circumstances she'd thought up had never been like this.

Jackson stood with his two guys and Gabe and all the shifters separated to transform on their own. Away from the others, she had to keep her mind on the task at hand. She couldn't worry about Kieran's reaction. If he rejected her jaguar, then she was sure they would never recover.

The past month wouldn't mean a thing. He would leave her, probably leave Las Vegas, and she would never see him again. That would actually be better than having to see him every day and not being able to touch him.

She started to undress, not really worrying about whether or not anyone was watching. As a young shifter, she'd learned early on that she couldn't always pick the time or place where she would transform.

It was one of the only lessons she'd learned from her family.

The Reese clan could be traced back to the beginning of time. Sure, the name changed, evolved, to fit into the world around them. But as one of the founding families of the Organization, they were proud of their history, so it was easy for Dakota to research.

It wasn't easy believing in what her company did while at the same time hating them for it.

From birth her mother and father had been cold and distant to her. Later, when her parents had given birth to her younger siblings, she hadn't understood why they accepted and loved the other children but not her.

Or she hadn't understood until her uncle, one she'd never seen before, who'd never been spoken of, had come to her house and told her about her destiny.

Destiny, she scoffed. She hadn't had a choice. As the first-born child, she belonged to the Organization, not her family.

When they'd thought she was ready, two men had arrived to take her away. She'd begged her parents to save her, not to let the man remove her from her home and family, but they'd turned their backs and allowed Dakota to be removed from the only home she'd ever known.

They'd rejected her.

If Kieran did the same, she wasn't certain she would ever recover. She'd made a family with the agents she'd grown up with and saw daily. Even then she'd kept herself removed from everyone else. Not to the extent of Kieran, but Dakota was very much alone.

Even Dean, who'd been her partner for years, had found it easy to leave her side and go hide in a lab every day. Their bond hadn't been enough to keep him with her.

So, really, what was she expecting from Kieran?

Of course he was going to end up leaving her. No one ever stayed.

"Stop!"

Dakota whirled around and almost stumbled. Kieran was only a few feet away. "What?"

"Stop thinking whatever you are," Kieran demanded. "I can sense something's wrong."

She'd already removed her shirt and pants and stood before him in only her bra and panties. "Yeah, sure."

"I mean it." He stepped closer. "This isn't going to change anything."

Oh, God, she really did want to believe him. "Okay."

"Stop telling me what you think I want to hear! Yell, scream, blame me! Question me!"

"We don't have time for this," she said, turning her back.

"I don't care." He grabbed her to spin her back around. "I'll admit I have doubts about myself."

"You lied to me earlier. You said you were sure we'd be okay, but you didn't mean it. Not really," she accused.

"Yes," Kieran said. "I'm worried I'll attack you."

"You wouldn't," she argued.

"I might," Kieran said. "Neither of us know what's going to happen in the next few minutes. But I have to believe, at least in my heart, nothing is going to change. That we'll get through this and be better for it."

Dakota blew out a breath. Okay, she needed to stop feeling sorry for herself. Her life wasn't bad, not really, and she had been so happy for the last month. At least she'd had that time with Kieran.

"Shift for me," Kieran urged.

Instead of moving away from him again, Dakota pulled off the rest of her clothes and crouched. She kept her gaze on Kieran as she called her jaguar forward.

The change washed over her with a familiar wave of power. She fell to the ground as her arms shortened then grew fur. The black spots stood out against the tan pelt on her back.

"Holy shit!" Kieran dropped to his knees in front of her.

Dakota had not expected that reaction. He was already reaching out toward her. She flattened herself to the ground, hoping if she wasn't showing any signs of aggression, he might come closer. She wanted his hand on her. She'd never felt his touch in her animal form.

"You're beautiful," he murmured.

She scooted forward a little, laying her chin on her paws.

"Can I touch you?" he asked.

They probably should have talked about that before she shifted. Dakota loved to be petted. She nodded her head, hoping he understood.

Kieran's first brush over her head was tentative, but when Dakota didn't move, he simply laid his palm on her. She closed her eyes and just breathed in relief. She wished,

wished so much, she could pull his scent into her and hold it forever, but he didn't have one. That had never bothered her before that moment.

"I'm not afraid or angry," Kieran said. "I know it's you."

She made a sound that would probably come across as a grunt and he laughed. Wow, she loved that sound. Even though they'd been together almost a month, she very rarely heard him laugh and it was usually during one of their fun and rowdy sex sessions.

"Everything okay?" Jackson called out.

Dakota wanted to roar at Jackson for interrupting them, but didn't want to scare Kieran. Instead she climbed onto her four paws and stretched out her back.

"Fine," Kieran hollered back. "Come on, kitten."

She took a swipe at him with her massive claw, but he stepped easily away. Around her the other shifters moved and her instincts kicked in.

With a roar, she leapt in front of Kieran, blocking him from a dark wolf that was stalking toward her lover. The wolf stopped with his ears pinned to his head and his teeth bared.

Dakota wasn't afraid. A jaguar could easily beat this wolf. She was bigger and meaner.

"No," Kieran said as he grabbed the scruff of her neck.

Dakota meowed before trying to get free. Why was he trying to protect the wolf? He was hers! She wasn't going to share him.

"You know Remy isn't going to hurt me," Kieran told her.

She shook her head to clear the animal craving to attack. She did know Remy wasn't a threat to Kieran, but she'd let herself forget about their mission and that wasn't acceptable.

When she tugged so he would release her, Kieran ran his hand over her head to her neck and patted.

She trotted away past the wolf and a bear and stopped in front of the largest fucking wolf she'd ever seen. As big and bad as she was, this wolf was an Alpha. She lowered herself into a crouch before she remembered she knew this wolf too. It had to be Damon.

It was unusual for her to get lost in her instincts as she was doing. She didn't know what was going on, but something was weird. The Alpha relaxed as soon as she did and dipped his head in her direction.

"Don't forget to check in," Jackson said as he stood next to the smaller wolf, Remy. "Call if you come across anything. If not, we'll meet back at the hotel."

"Mine and Dakota's room would be best," Kieran said. "Hunt as long as you can, but be safe and don't use all your energy. If we find them, we have to get everyone out safely."

"Let's go find us some bad guys," Jackson said.

Dakota watched the other teams separate, leaving her with Kieran and the Alpha.

"We've got the north section," Kieran said. "Try to keep up."

Dakota didn't understand until Kieran used his Walker speed and was gone. She grunted before taking off after him.

Her paws barely hit the hard ground as she ran at full tilt. She could catch sight of him, but since she knew what direction he was headed in, she was able to really give the jaguar the freedom she rarely got anymore.

Running in the city was regulated for the safety of shifters and humans. She still got to transform, but with other types of animals around, she couldn't trust one not to attack her.

Her natural tendency was to remain solitary except with her mate. She didn't like to pick up the scents of others. Here, with Kieran so close, she was safe to enjoy the wind mussing her fur, and not holding back.

Ahead she heard Kieran's laughter and knew he was taunting her. So he thought he could beat her? Yeah, right. She spotted a tree that would take her up into the caverns of the mountain. Her jaguar might not be the best climber of the large felines, but she did okay. She really excelled in water, but there was none to be found around here.

Dakota didn't even slow as she reached the tree. Instead she leapt and landed on one of the thick branches. She ascended as far as she could until only a small gap between her and the ledge remained. She balanced for an instant then jumped, but landed exactly where she wanted. From the vantage point, she could see down below, where the wolf was scrambling to catch up. Where the hell was Kieran?

"Over here, kitten."

Dakota swiveled around to see Kieran leaning against the mountain face with his arms crossed over his chest. She roared playfully at his nickname for her. She had a feeling it was going to stick.

Chapter Five

Kieran couldn't believe that, instead of fear at Dakota's roar, he was turned on by the sound. His life was just getting more and more complicated. Behind Dakota, the Alpha finally joined them.

"I found our first cave," Kieran announced. "From here on out we need to be silent."

Both animals nodded. Kieran grinned. Maybe he'd get Dakota to shift more often. He liked her not being able to argue. He spun on his heel and headed in the direction of the opening he'd seen a couple of minutes before.

The jaguar and wolf moved almost silently as they followed. They were far enough away from the opening he'd seen that they didn't really have to be quiet yet, but it was better since they didn't know if the group they were searching for had guards. If they were smart, they would.

Kieran used enough speed to move them quickly, but made sure both shifters were able to keep up with him. When he found what he was looking for, he crouched and waited. Dakota licked his arm when she reached him.

"Let me go in first," he told them. "You two stay at the opening. I can move faster and if no one is inside, then we can move on. If I think I'm not alone, I'll call out for you."

The Alpha gave a low growl and Kieran took it he didn't like that plan.

"I doubt they have any Walkers working for them," Kieran said. "Most shifters won't even see me and we know they can't smell me."

Dakota butted her head against his leg. It was amazing he was so close to the jaguar. He took her broad head in his hands and kissed her snout. She wrinkled her nose and it was so cute he smiled at her.

"I'll be back before you know it," he promised.

Kieran climbed to his feet and raced away. The gap in the mountain was about half his height and it would be hard to get people in and out, but that didn't mean the shifter group didn't enter in their animal form or use this as an emergency exit. He couldn't take chances even if he didn't think he was going to find anyone inside.

The rocks under his feet crumbled and he slipped as he dropped down to his knees. He couldn't believe he was crawling through a damn hole taking him into the dark. He fucking hated the dark.

It seemed like an hour, although it couldn't have been more than five minutes, before he broke through the tunnel. If he didn't have Walker vision, he wasn't sure he would have been able to see the small amount he could. It was pitch-black.

Kieran placed his hand on the wall as he stood. There were no noises echoing around. He was even more certain this wasn't going to lead anywhere, but he had to check. He slid his palm over the rough side of the mountain to keep his bearings.

As he headed deeper into the shadows, it got colder and Kieran grew uncomfortable. He clenched his eyes tightly and tried to take deep breaths. He could feel his mind slipping back into the memories. He tried to fight them, but he knew he wouldn't be able to.

Kieran was sure this time he was going to die. He was strapped to a chair instead of a table. Every finger had been broken, his right hand smashed, and he'd suffered one of the worst beatings he'd gotten. The worst was they'd ripped out his fangs, again.

"Why?" he managed to ask through his swollen mouth.

The cackle sent a chill down his spine. "Because I can."

That was the answer he always got when he asked the question. He didn't know how long he'd been held captive, but he was certain it had to be into years by now.

"You do heal remarkably well," the doctor told him.

Kieran had no idea if the man really was a doctor, but that was what he called the hyena shifter. He loved to poke and prod Kieran as well as inject unknown substances. Kieran had figured out a long time ago they were testing him to see what he could and could not heal from. There were instances when they even gave him blood so his healing was sped up. Whatever suited their purposes at that moment.

But he hadn't had any blood for so long Kieran knew he was slowly dying. He had prayed the night before, alone and freezing in his cage, for his body to just give up.

He wasn't immortal, but he was damn hard to kill. The shifters were close to ending him though.

"I've gotten more data from you than any of my other test subjects. Now I'm just trying to see how long you can last. It's quite entertaining," the doctor mused.

Kieran was in so much pain he couldn't even flinch when the doctor held a scalpel in front of him.

"I do love to hear you scream, though," the shifter told him.

He'd tried, he really had, but he did scream as the scalpel pierced his chest and set up a burning from the inside.

"I treated the blade with a little something special for you," the hyena doctor said.

Kieran gritted his teeth and his vision wavered.

"I think I'll return you to your cell. I'll check on you in about twenty-four hours. See if you're still alive."

Kieran found himself on his knees gasping. The vision or memory was one of the strongest he'd suffered. It was also a reminder of one the worst nights of his life.

Whatever the doctor had given him had eaten away at his insides as he lay curled up in his cage. He'd screamed. Begged them to kill him, but no one ever came. Not until days later.

Kieran hadn't been able to even raise his head when the shifters had picked him up and carried him into a filthy washing area. They'd dropped him onto the stained, broken tiles before turning on a hose with cold water above him.

He hadn't been warm after that until his rescue. Even the blood they'd given him hadn't heated him at all.

Bile rose and he lurched to the side before he vomited. Shit, this couldn't be happening. He was finally happy and the memories were going to tear him apart.

No, he wouldn't let them. He was stronger than some fucked-up past. He'd made himself strong. He would never be a victim again, wouldn't have to rely on another to rescue him. Kieran did the rescuing now and he was going to do his damn job.

He climbed to his feet and rolled his shoulders. He was done cowering. It was time to bring Bradley and the other shifters to their knees. The doctor had never been found. Maybe once he found Alex, that was what he would do. Track down the fucker.

It was time he was in charge of his own life again. For months, he'd let everyone dictate what was happening with him. Caspar had maneuvered him into coming to Las Vegas. He was working for Sparro just so he could keep in contact with Caspar and even being around Jackson was bringing up these painful memories. *No more!* He was in control of his life and it was time he proved it.

Determination had him moving forward to check out this cave and move on to the next.

* * * *

Dakota was filthy, hot and exhausted. It had been a long day of tracking in and out of caves and one that hadn't brought them any closer to finding Alex or the other missing shifters. The hours had taken a toll on them emotionally as well.

After the first time Kieran had left to search by himself, he'd grown quiet and cold. He'd still petted her once he returned, but his touch was different, distant somehow, and she didn't know why.

Once they'd had to call it a day, almost ten hours after

they'd started, Kieran had called Jackson and it had been decided everyone would clean up and meet back in their suite for food and updates. Even the Alpha was coming into town.

It didn't appear Damon was going to let them keep him out of the investigation.

She couldn't say she was really surprised. If it were her, she'd want to know what was happening. It didn't help that the first agents in charge of the case had royally screwed up. And the Alpha was coming in handy.

It had become obvious right from the start there was no way Kieran could search all the hidden openings by himself. There were just too many. Damon had shifted back to human form and argued with Kieran that they would have to split up. Dakota hadn't liked that idea. At least guarding the entrances she would have been able to run to his defense if he'd found trouble, but Damon was right. She'd let the two males decide and finally Kieran had seen reason.

"You okay?" she asked her lover as they stepped into the hotel.

"Just tired and frustrated," he replied.

Dakota knew it was more than that, but she didn't push. The others had left before them so there wasn't a whole lot of time to get cleaned up before they arrived.

"I'm going to take a shower. Want to join me?"

"Go ahead," Kieran said as he strolled across the room to the desk. "I want to check my email, then I'll come wash your back."

She held in a sigh but made her way to the bathroom by herself.

Even the sight of the freshly made bed with all the extra blankets and pillows didn't bring her any happiness. She was worried about Kieran. This entire investigation was tearing him apart. She could see it in the dullness of his blue eyes as well as in the circles underneath.

She wanted to suggest he take blood from her but was

scared it would end up in a fight.

Kieran had told her from the beginning he didn't want to drink from her. Dakota still didn't understand. Kieran kept control and would never hurt her. He needed only a few sips from her every few weeks and could go a month. As far as she knew, he hadn't had any blood since she'd convinced him in the very beginning of their relationship she wanted to try.

It hadn't been anything like she'd thought.

He'd told her it wasn't like a Hollywood movie, but she'd still romanticized the act. Instead he said he never drank from the throat but preferred the wrist. He also wouldn't touch her sexually as he drank. He'd had so many rules, but in the end she'd understood.

Being fed on by a Walker was not a pleasant experience for a human. They would grow sick, the illness in Kieran passing on to them, and they would throw up and have flu-like symptoms for several days.

Shifters handled it better, though.

She'd only had a small headache, which had quickly gone away once Kieran had lain his body over hers and made her very, *very* happy. She smiled, thinking about how he'd loved her fast and hard before being gentle and caring. He was so damn complicated, but that was what made him unique. Made her want to protect him from all the bad things out there. Which was absolutely ridiculous, since he was a Walker and one of the strongest creatures in the world.

Still, she got to see him unlike anyone else. The vulnerability he couldn't hide, though he tried, in such close quarters all the time.

Dakota began to strip as soon as she walked into the bathroom. A hot shower would clear her head and take away some of the weariness she was feeling. Hopefully Kieran would indeed come and wash her back.

She turned on the water as hot as she would be able to stand it before she climbed inside the huge stall. "Ahh," she groaned as the heat soaked into her neck while the water pounded down. She really wished Kieran had joined her. He would need this too.

As she closed her eyes and rolled her shoulders, the bathroom door opened and a waft of cool air drifted in before it clicked back closed. At least it hadn't taken him all night.

"You look so beautiful like that," he said.

Dakota turned and saw him eying her body.

"I bet I'd feel even better," she teased. She held out a hand to him and was relieved when he immediately took it before crowding her against the warm tiles. He ran his hands down her slick body as she cupped his face.

He still looked tired, but whatever mood he'd been in seemed to have passed for the moment. She rose to her tiptoes and kissed him, deep and dirty.

Their tongues dueled until she gave in and he took control. As soon as she submitted, she was rewarded by him lifting her up off the ground with her back plastered to the tiles.

Every touch of his hands over her body heightened her arousal until she was pushing her breasts against him in a silent plea for more.

Kieran drew his mouth back and she chased those delicious lips. "I want to taste you," he said.

"Yes, please."

He lowered her feet back down to the floor then dropped to his knees while running his tongue over her stomach and down.

Dakota moaned and gripped the back of his head. "I need you so badly."

"I know," he said before trailing his palm up her leg then positioning her with her knee over his shoulder. "Open up for me."

Like she could have resisted him? Or would want to.

The first sweep of his tongue between her folds had her shivering, but when he added his fingers along with his tongue inside her pussy, she almost came apart.

He fingered and licked her at a brutal pace that had her orgasm threatening sooner than she would have liked. With every hump of her hips, she rode out the delirious rush.

"That's it," he murmured. "Show me how much you want me."

"Always," she panted. "Always want you." Oh, God, she could feel her body getting ready to explode. She wanted to watch him on his knees in front of her, but she couldn't keep her eyes open. She trembled, her clit tingled and she dropped her head back.

He plunged a third finger into her as he sucked hard on her clit.

Dakota screamed as she climaxed. Kieran kept rubbing her until she started to fall.

"I'm not done with you yet," he said helping her to steady on her shaking legs. "Bend over the seat."

Since she was still too clumsy to comply, Kieran used his hands on top of hers to get them braced on the built-in ledge. He gripped her hips and pulled her back to where she could feel his hard cock stroke between her thighs. Dakota spread her legs farther apart, inviting him to take her.

He pressed his hand against her entrance right before he plunged his shaft in deep. Hissing, she raised to her toes as he drove forward. It felt so fucking good. The pleasure made everything else disappear. She couldn't feel the water raining down on them anymore. Had no idea if it was still hot or if it'd grown cold.

Kieran was still holding her tightly as he withdrew.

Was he bigger? No, there was no way. It just felt as if he was filling her more than ever before. She knew that in her mind, but her body was having trouble remembering all the other times they'd been together.

It felt like the first time. That intense connection sizzling between them.

He growled then thrust hard. Dakota gasped. He did it again.

"I won't break," she told him. "Fuck me hard." She

needed to see some of that control of his vanish. To know she could make him just as crazy as she felt.

"Mine," he whispered against her ear.

She nodded frantically. "Prove it."

The pounding rhythm he'd started had her entire body rocking forward and she pushed desperately back against him. Sweat dripped off her forehead into her eyes, but she couldn't move her hands to brush the moisture off her face or she would have ended up falling.

Every drive of his cock had Kieran grunting and she knew her lover was close. She clamped her inner muscles down on his shaft and he yelled and cursed. Dakota grinned. She wasn't going to last much longer and, damn it, he wasn't going over the edge with her. When Kieran's hips started to stutter and his grasp slipped, she took the chance and reached her left arm back to hold him close.

He came, howling her name and filling her with cum. Heat took her over from the inside out and it was marvelous. Kieran didn't stop his thrusts until her own orgasm was triggered and this time she did collapse.

Kieran caught her and how he managed when he was shaking as badly as she was, she didn't know, but she did appreciate it.

"Fuck," he said between puffs of air, trying to catch his breath.

"Oh my God," Dakota replied. "I don't think I can walk. I can't feel my feet."

His soft rumble of laughter brushed over her cheek as he rested his lips on her temple. "Let me wash you. I don't think you have time for a nap, though, so stay awake."

She whined. It wasn't something she would ever admit out loud, but when he moved her under the showerhead, she actually whined. It wasn't that she was opposed to being clean, but he was right. It would at least be several hours until they would be alone again.

When he'd soaped up and rinsed every part of her, twice, Dakota gingerly climbed out of the shower to let him finish up. Luckily, they'd had plenty of hot water.

The mirror was fogged up, so after she'd dried off and wrapped her towel around her body, she wiped off the condensation. Kieran's reflection was distorted, but she would never get tired of looking at him.

The scars from his years of torture stood out against his wet, pale skin.

He hated them and had once told her she was the only person he'd ever let touch the marks. Dakota wished they weren't there, but for Kieran's sake, not hers. To her the damage that had been inflicted on him should be visible. It showed he had survived. That he hadn't let the monsters win. It wouldn't be right for there not to be physical evidence of what he'd endured.

Kieran turned off the taps and the bathroom grew quiet as he reached out to scoop up his own towel.

Distantly she could hear someone else in the suite. It sounded like the noise came from the living area. She should go out there and help set up the food, but instead she waited until Kieran stood beside her, wiping off the drops of water clinging to his broad chest.

"Don't look at me like that," he told her. "We don't have time for another round."

"We could always ignore them and hope they go away?" she suggested.

"When have you known that to work on Remy?" he asked playfully.

"Shit." She had to agree with him there. Remy would probably want to set up a video camera or something. Kieran's partner was a very odd duck...wolf...whatever.

"Come on." Kieran took her hand and tugged her to the door. "Let's get dressed."

"Wait." She pulled him back.

Kieran glanced down at her. "What is it?"

"I wanted... We didn't talk about..." She blew out a breath. "Shit! Are you sure you're okay with seeing my jaguar today?"

He laughed. At first she wasn't sure whether she should be insulted or not. But he grabbed her hips and lifted her to sit on the vanity before moving in between her legs. He cupped her face before pushing back her neck so she was gazing up at him.

"As shocked as I am to say it, yes. I am so glad I got to see your jaguar."

"Really?"

"I promise."

"You didn't freak out."

"Actually, I had the opposite reaction. I was a little turned on by seeing you in your animal form," Kieran confessed.

She blinked up at him, unsure how to respond.

"Now don't get me wrong," he said. "There won't be any bestiality or anything like that. I like you human and…you. But seeing you like that was powerful."

"I'm so relieved," she admitted.

"Me too," he agreed. "I can't say I understand why. I'm still wary of Remy when he's in wolf form, but it was different from you. I had to touch you. Not to make me feel better to know it was you. I'm as drawn to you in your jaguar form as I as in your human one, it seems."

"You know," she teased, "I love to be petted in my other form." She wrapped her legs around the back of his.

"You love to be stroked in any form," he replied.

"True. If you're the one doing the petting."

His hard-on pushed against the fabric of the towel. She reached down and ran her fingers lightly over his shaft.

"We could practice caressing and fondling in your human form and…"

The pounding on the bathroom door startled them. Kieran jumped back and she almost fell off the counter.

"Remy! God damn it!" Kieran yelled.

"Just wanted to make sure you knew we were here. I don't really feel like hearing round two!" Remy called back.

"I'm going to kill him," Kieran threatened.

Remy's laughter could be heard clearly through the door.

"Go away, Remy," Dakota shouted. "Or I'm going to let him hurt you this once."

"Fine!" Mirth was still obvious in his voice. "But seriously, food's here. And I'm not waiting on you to eat."

"We're coming," she hollered back.

"Not now we're not," Kieran muttered as he fixed the towel around his waist.

"Did you just make a sex joke?" she asked. She pushed him to the side and hopped off the vanity. "You bad boy!"

"I'll show you bad and not care who hears!" He reached for her, but, laughing, Dakota avoided him and opened the bathroom door. She was glad that Remy had left the bedroom and closed the door behind him.

"I could have had you if I really wanted," Kieran told her with a pout.

"Just get dressed. I smell steak," she ordered.

"Fine," he bitched but he did head toward his dresser. "I've been passed over for a steak."

"And wine," she added. "A whole lot of wine."

Dakota strolled over to the bed then flopped down and knew it had been a mistake. Christ! The bed was so damn comfortable. She just wanted to lie back and...

"Here!"

She looked up to get a pile of clothes in the face. "What was that for?"

"You were thinking about lying down and you said you were hungry. We skipped lunch and, with the shifting, that is not good for you."

"Are you taking care of me?" she asked sweetly as she rose to her feet.

"Someone needs to." He'd already pulled on a pair of soft black sweatpants and was currently tugging on a dark blue knit sweater. She loved him in black leather and his bad-boy get-up, but when he was laid-back and dressed for comfort, she just wanted to devour him.

"Stop!" He pointed his finger at her.

Dakota grinned in response, but decided he wasn't going

to let her play anymore while they had guests, so she might as well stop torturing the both of them. He'd tossed her a pair of worn blue lounge pants and a white V-neck T-shirt that were both warm and snuggly, so she quickly clothed herself. He waited at the door and took her hand before pulling it open.

It looked like everyone else had already arrived. The table was covered with plates and platters of food while their guests had made themselves comfortable.

Dean, Gabe and Dare sat with their backs to the wall and plates on their laps. Remy, Jackson and Damon were all settled in the living room chairs and were using the coffee table for their dishes. That left the couch for her and Kieran.

Next to Jackson's chair, a younger man sat, and by the lack of scent he had to be a Walker. He also appeared to be much younger than anyone else in the room. Not that it was easy to guess a Walker's age. They might not be immortal, but they lived a long damn time.

Still, if Jackson had brought him to this meeting, the kid must be important.

"Where's the wine?" she asked as they stepped in the room.

Remy held up a bottle. "It's the good stuff too. Jackson doesn't skimp."

She took it as they strolled past. There was still plenty of food left and no doubt the shifters at least would be making another trip to the buffet to fuel up. It really did take a lot of energy to shift and stay in their animal form for as long as they did.

"Pour the wine and I'll bring the plates," Kieran told her.

That worked for her. She caught up two of the crystal glasses and made her way back to the others. There wasn't much talking as everyone devoured their dinners. She poured both her and Kieran some of the red wine before passing it back over to Remy, who refilled his and Damon's glasses.

It was the largest group she and Kieran had entertained,

but she enjoyed the feel of those in the room with her. Walkers, shifters and humans all seemed to blend well together.

"This is my IT guy, Mitch Anderson." Jackson patted the kid's shoulder. "He and Dean worked so well together I thought it would be a good idea for them to meet and maybe cook up some more plans."

"He's brilliant," Dean said through a mouthful of food. "Better than me even."

"That's high praise," Dakota commented before taking a sip of her drink.

The kid blushed, which she wouldn't have thought possible for a Walker. He appeared to be in his early twenties. The tips of his black hair were dyed bright blue and he had ratty jeans on. If she was to see him on the streets, she wouldn't have pegged him as working for one of the most powerful men in the city.

"I'm happy to help," Mitch told her. "I just want to find Alex."

She nodded. "We do too."

Kieran rejoined them and handed her a plate before he sat next to her. The smell of the steak, baked potatoes, green beans and fresh rolls had her mouth watering already.

Jackson wiped his mouth with his napkin and settled back in his chair. "I let my other guys head home for a while to rest. They'd been up for over thirty-six hours."

"So have you," Kieran pointed out. Dakota could hear the concern in her lover's voice.

"I feel better now I've showered, but I'll catch some sleep when I can. I did get full reports from my men before I let them go," Jackson said. "Unless you would like your agents to do the honors?"

Both Dare and Gabe waved him off as they continued to demolish their food.

"Guess not," Jackson said with a laugh.

"Why don't you start with your update first then," Dakota suggested. "They can add anything they need during their sections."

"Here, I brought this." Dean jumped to his feet and hurried to the other side of the room, where the office was.

She hadn't even noticed the rolling boards, extra computers, or boxes when she'd entered. Dean pushed one of the boards over—it had a copy of a map pinned to it.

"I circled the sections that were divided up today and figured we could just cross out what we've already eliminated," Dean said.

"Good idea," Jackson agreed as he stood. He strolled over to Dean and accepted the marker Dean handed him. "We've been able to reduce the areas we searched today, but what worries me is no one saw any sign of traffic. No vehicle tracks, footprints or anything. It makes me question if we're completely off-base."

He started to X out most of the map.

"I had that thought myself," Damon said. "But even though we never found a sign of them, I can't get over the feeling that we were closer than we thought."

Jackson and Damon both looked toward Kieran. Dakota shifted in her seat so she could better see him as well. What was she missing?

"You felt it too?" Kieran asked quietly.

"What?" she and Remy questioned together.

Kieran turned his gaze to her. "Evil, there was a sense of evil around that place. It might be from something that happened long ago, but it's just a feeling I had about halfway through."

She nodded even though she couldn't really say she understood. What did evil feel like? she wanted to ask, but that was a conversation for later.

"I agree," Damon stated, drawing her attention. "I'm used to the area. I showed you where we run, but I've never sensed the wrongness in the mountains like I did today."

"It wasn't until the end for me," Jackson said, pointing with his marker. "The closer to where my section butted up with yours."

Kieran sat his plate on the coffee table before he stood. Dakota noticed the humans and the shifters in the room looked just as confused as she felt. Her lover took the marker from Jackson and made his own addition to the map. "This is where all the teams need to concentrate."

"It still looks like a pretty good-size area," Dakota commented.

"Yeah," Kieran agreed. "But we might get a better sense of things when we get there."

"We should go now." Jackson grabbed Kieran's arm.

"No," Kieran replied gently.

"What?" Jackson shouted. "If it was you—"

"I'd want you to wait until it was safe," Kieran interrupted. "No one has gotten any sleep. The shifters need to gain their energy back."

"Then I'll take my own people," Jackson insisted.

"Who haven't slept either. Probably haven't fed as well. If we're not one hundred percent prepared when we find where they're hiding, they'll kill Alex and anyone else they have." Kieran gripped Jackson's shoulder and pulled him in. "I know you don't want him to suffer, but we have to be smart about this. They haven't had Alex as long as they had us. They won't have him as long."

Jackson nodded and seemed to deflate. Kieran held his old friend and Dakota wished she had something to offer him as well. Kieran was absolutely correct. If they rushed in without a plan, they would end up getting themselves killed or captured.

She was surprised when Damon stood and walked over to Jackson.

"Today was a good day. We were able to get closer than I thought we would. We have a solid idea of where they might be," Damon said. "Going in at dawn, we'll be refreshed and ready."

"Alex is strong," Mitch told Jackson from his spot on the ground. "You know he'd agree with your friends."

"Okay." Jackson lifted up his hands. "Okay."

Kieran led Jackson back to the chair, so Dakota looked over at Dean. "Were you able to find out anything else?"

"Mitch has been searching the database they keep when paranormals enter the city," Dean responded. "I'm not even going to go into how illegal that is, by the way."

"What database?" Mitch asked with a grin.

Dean glanced at him before turning back to her and rolling his eyes. "See? It's nearly impossible to work with Walkers."

"Hey!" Mitch complained.

"*Anyway*," Dean drawled. "He thinks he has some possible suspects who arrived and were never spotted again."

"Email me the files," Kieran told him.

Mitch glanced at Jackson who nodded his permission. "Sure," Mitch agreed.

"Anything else?" Kieran asked.

"We still can't find Alex's car," Dean said.

"I'm not really surprised," Kieran told him. "They never found my truck either."

Dakota hadn't known that. She barely remembered that was how they'd captured him in the first place.

"The best plan is to have two teams," Remy told the group. "The search team we'll make up and a backup of agents in case we do find them."

"My Pack can serve as backup as well," Damon offered.

"We still need to keep this as legal as possible," Dean said. "Especially with the Coalition sniffing around."

"Was that a shifter joke?" Remy asked Dean.

"If the collar fits," Dean answered with a smile.

"That was pretty good. The collar remark too," Remy told him. "Kieran must be rubbing off on you."

Dean might not have paled, but he came pretty damn close to causing everyone to laugh and break the tension.

"This is what we do," Remy said once he had all their attention again. "How we end this once and for all."

Chapter Six

Alex couldn't even lift his head any longer but that didn't stop the sadistic shifters from pummeling his face.

He hurt everywhere. He was pretty sure several of his bones and ribs were broken and he was losing blood at an alarming rate.

To his horror, he'd been right before, when he'd thought whoever had him were the same men who had taken Kieran and Jackson so many years ago. So he knew this was just the beginning. He had seen the scars over Jackson's body when they worked out together. Alex had known things had been bad, but experiencing them was a whole different matter.

It took a lot to get a Walker or shifter to scar. Most of the time the healing ability would take care of the marks, but a body, even a paranormal, could only take so much.

He heard the door open and a couple of new footsteps join them, but he was past caring how many people were present for his torture.

"This is the Walker?"

Alex didn't recognize the voice, but that didn't mean the guy hadn't been responsible for beating on him. His neck was jerked back by a hand in his hair and he grunted.

"I don't think he'll last as long as the other two we had all those years ago. It'll do for now, but don't forget you promised to get me back the ones I lost."

This time Alex knew it was the man everyone called Doc speaking. He'd told him with each new torment how Jackson and Kieran had responded. Alex didn't claim to be as strong as the other two Walkers. He wished he hadn't even felt a sliver of what they had.

The doctor and the newcomer both crouched in front of him.

"Pity, this one won't make it," the newcomer said, slapping Alex's face hard a couple of times. "I always love to see you work with the vampires. And I know what I promised you."

Alex wanted to snarl and say he wasn't a vampire, but he didn't have the energy. What did it matter what this madman called him? The doctor was right—he wasn't going to last as long as Jackson or Kieran had. He already wanted his pain to end.

"Do you know who I am?" the newcomer asked Alex.

He blinked in reply.

"No?" The laugh was chilling. "Your boss didn't tell you about his old friend Bradley who he spent so much time with? How about Kieran? Did he mention me?"

Fuck, fuck, fuck. He knew that name. In front of him was the shifter every Organization agent was after. Jackson had given Kieran access to all the files they had on this guy.

He had lost his mind some years ago and was convinced he could find out what made the Walkers live longer than shifters. Both had extended years of life compared to humans, but apparently Bradley wasn't happy with the time he'd been given.

"Ah." Bradley smiled. "So you do know me. My feelings were about to be hurt. I've just arrived, plane delayed, but I do hope you'll be a little more entertaining than the shifters I've been getting videos of. Doc enjoys his work so much, but this time around I think we are wasting our time with the shifters. I thought it might be worth seeing the difference between your species and mine, but I was mistaken. The animals here just can't stand this kind of experiment. Weaklings, all of them. I should have taken an Alpha."

"You're sick," Alex mumbled. His words were slurred, but he hoped he got his disgust across.

"Possibly," Bradley replied. Then he turned toward the doctor. "Please proceed. I'd like a show before I hit the town."

The doctor's eyes lit up. "I've been saving this part for you." He disappeared out of Alex's sight for a moment, but when he returned he held pliers in one hand and a bottle of blood in the other.

"No!" Alex groaned. He knew what was going to happen. Jackson had told him stories about this.

"Oh yes," the doctor said as he waved the bottle of blood under Alex's nose.

He tried. He closed his eyes, turned his head, bucked in his seat, but the smell of the blood was too strong. His fangs dropped down and his mouth was wrenched open.

The doctor placed the pliers in his mouth. "Smile pretty!"

Alex screamed as his left fang was ripped from his gums. Blood filled his mouth and he wondered if he would choke on it. His vision started to darken and he didn't fight it. Maybe if he passed out, they would leave him alone.

Tears were running down his face as the doctor latched on to his right fang.

"I love to see them suffer," Bradley said just as the doctor pulled.

He'd never felt pain like that before in his life. He'd been shot, stabbed, burned, but never had he felt this…this agony.

* * * *

Four hours of sleep. That was all Kieran had managed, but he was thinking it would be enough. It was probably more than Jackson was getting too. The events of the day were almost a guarantee they wouldn't be sleeping easy for some time. He was going to have to decide what to do about his insomnia, but he had bigger worries at the moment.

In just a few short hours, they'd be going back out to the Red Rocks and Kieran had a feeling they were going to find what they were looking for and more. The thought filled him with just as much dread as it did relief. He wanted to find Alex and the others, but he wasn't looking forward to seeing what had been done to them.

It would all be worth it in the end if they could catch these bastards this time. But Kieran doubted that was going to be possible. Every other operation that had them close to tracking down Bradley and his group had ended up with them arriving just days or even hours after the place had been abandoned. It was one of the reasons he'd almost agreed with Jackson earlier about going right away.

But he'd seen the exhaustion and strain on his friend's face and knew no one in the room was ready.

He couldn't risk Dakota, Remy or any of them in a fight as big as this. He needed to feed and knew Jackson had to as well. Hopefully his friend was taking advantage of the donors he kept on staff. Jackson had offered them to Kieran, but he always preferred to hunt for his own dinner.

That was why he was dressed in all black as he snuck out of the bedroom. Dakota probably wouldn't say anything if she knew what he planned, but he hadn't wanted to risk it. Her first instinct would always be to offer herself and Kieran avoided that conversation as much as he could.

He hated that he had to take someone's blood. That the disease inside him that gave him his unique traits also kept him reliant on another. It was part of his life and he accepted what he had to do, but he didn't want to involve Dakota.

Kieran strolled over to his laptop for a quick check before he headed out. There were several new emails, but the last one had him sitting down and pulling the computer closer. It was from Caspar and the subject line said *BE CAREFUL*.

He double-clicked on the message.

We tracked Bradley to Vegas. He was on a private flight that landed earlier this evening. We lost him at the airport. He knows you and Jackson are there. I'm on my way. Don't do anything without me.

Kieran forwarded the email to Jackson with his own message.

We're still on for dawn.

He was warning his friend, but he knew Jackson wouldn't want to wait any longer than Kieran did.

Caspar shouldn't be in the fight in the first place. If they could catch Bradley before Caspar arrived, then his boss would remain safe. He would have to digest the information about Bradley knowing where he was. It really should have dawned on him earlier that Bradley would be able to find Jackson easily enough. Jackson didn't hide himself and was well-known around the world for the hotels and casinos he'd built.

If anyone was watching Jackson, then Kieran would have been found as well.

It just hadn't crossed his mind that he'd put himself and Dakota at risk. True, he'd figured on Bradley being on the run, but Kieran should have known better.

He needed to get out of there.

Kieran stood, ignoring the rest of the emails. He would check them once he got back, but he had to go now. The need to run, to hunt was burning inside him with the rage of just hearing Bradley's name. He strolled through the living room and out of the door. His fangs had already dropped and he was going to find someone who deserved to be on the bad side of him tonight.

The elevator took too damn long and Kieran fidgeted until the doors opened. He practically ran out. The casino was a lot quieter this time of morning than usual but still no one bothered him as his long strides took him across the lobby and to the doors.

The lights remained bright in the valet area, but he didn't head to get his pickup or his motorcycle. Instead he strolled casually around the hotel building that would lead him onto the Strip. There were lots of alleys he could hunt in until someone deserved his attention.

It was actually quite a walk through the large parking area of the hotel until he reached the sidewalk. By the time he hit the street, he'd already calmed down. He still wanted to hunt, but his fangs had gone back inside his gums and he was once again in control.

"Going for a walk?"

Kieran shook his head before turning around. "You should be in bed."

Jackson laughed. "Really? I'd be there alone. You have a sexy little shifter warming your spot."

Kieran growled at him.

"Hey," Jackson shrugged. "I'm just pointing out the facts."

"How'd you know I left?" Kieran asked.

"You walked right past me. I figured I had better follow you to make sure you didn't get yourself in trouble. If you hadn't seen me, you wouldn't have seen an attack either."

"No one was going to attack me inside."

"After the email you just sent me I wouldn't be so sure. Bradley is just crazy enough to try to take one of us from my place," Jackson pointed out.

Kieran blew out a breath, frustrated that Jackson was right.

"So where are we headed?" Jackson asked.

"You're going back into the hotel and trying to get some sleep." Kieran pointed behind Jackson. "I'm going hunting."

Jackson rubbed his hands together. "I haven't hunted in years."

"And you're not going to tonight."

"Well, I'm not letting you go alone."

"You don't hunt anymore. Your face is too recognizable. If someone spotted you, your secret would be out."

"I can handle it," Jackson insisted. "Besides, it might do me some good to get my hands dirty. I miss the adrenaline rush. It's not the same as paying someone to feed from."

"You can't kill anyone," Kieran ordered. He didn't kill

anymore and couldn't let Jackson do so. He was an agent, after all. Plus, Dakota wouldn't like it.

"I know." Jackson waved him off. "We've both gone legit."

Kieran snorted. He might have cleaned up his act some, but he was still far from legit. "Let's go."

Jackson nodded before falling into step with Kieran. They were both dressed in dark clothing and both were big guys. No one smart would attempt to target them for a mugging or anything, so they'd have to find someone already committing a crime.

As Kieran led Jackson away from tourists and into the darker part of town, the city noises were muted, making it easier for them to hear for a couple of blocks.

"You do this often?" Jackson asked quietly.

Kieran glanced over to his friend. "Not as much as I used to."

"Because of Dakota?"

"Not the only reason, but she's probably a big part," Kieran admitted. "Even after all she's seen being with the Organization, she still believes in people. Sees the good in the world. I try to keep her away from the dark places. Even if that's where I'm most comfortable."

"From everything I've heard and seen, she's a very capable agent."

Kieran shrugged. "I guess I just don't want her to see me in that environment."

"I can understand that. That kid tonight, Mitch, the one who works in my IT."

"Yeah?"

"He has to be the most innocent kid I've ever met," Jackson said. "He'd been kicked around the foster system. Dragged from one group home to another. Never in one spot for long, and no family would take a teenager."

"How'd you come across him?"

"He hacked into one of my arcade games in the kids' area." Jackson laughed. "Fixed it up so he could stay inside all night and play. It'd been snowing for days and he didn't have anywhere to sleep."

Kieran smiled. "So you found him a job."

"Some food, a shower and a soft bed. He'd been feeding on small animals. Thought he'd lose control and kill a human if he bit them."

"No one ever showed him how to feed?" Kieran asked, shocked.

"No," Jackson answered. "He actually thought he was a vampire. His fangs would drop down and he'd find a stray cat or dog. He said he never killed them and would nurse them back to health when he could. At one of the group homes, he'd refused to go outside because he thought he'd burst into flames. They beat him and threw him into the yard. Mitch found out the sun didn't hurt him, but it confused him even more."

"Fuck, that had to be rough."

"Yeah, but I come across him playing vintage Pac Man and he didn't try to attack or anything. Just dropped his head and apologized. When I offered him food and a bed, he thought I was trying to buy him," Jackson shared. "It took me hours to convince him I didn't want sex in trade. He hadn't done that yet, but knew boys who had. With the weather so bad, it was a thought he'd been having."

"Good thing you found him when you did," Kieran said and meant it. It sounded like Mitch had had as bad a childhood as Kieran's adult life. At least he'd had his family until he was eighteen.

"As soon as I showed him I was a Walker too, he asked about a thousand questions. I had to bring in Alex just so I could get a break," Jackson continued. "He hasn't left our side since. Alex found out he was a genius, a real one, and we put him in school."

"I'd say it worked out for all involved. If Dean was impressed, then the kid knows his shit."

"And still he is innocent. He asked me if we were going to kill Bradley and the others that took Alex."

"If luck is on our side," Kieran commented.

"That's what I said," Jackson replied. "I thought he'd want to hear that the people responsible for taking Alex would be punished."

"He doesn't?" Kieran asked surprised.

"Oh he wants them caught, but he asked me if we could just hurt them a little."

"He said that?" Kieran was now amused.

"Yeah," Jackson replied. "We want them to pay but..." He shook his head. "Christ, man, I didn't know what to tell him. If I get my hands on Bradley or the doctor, or anyone really, I don't know if I'll be able to hold back."

"I know," Kieran agreed. He'd had the same thought earlier. He didn't think Dakota or Remy would try to stop him. They knew what he'd suffered, but that didn't mean he wanted them to see how he would handle them.

"The kid..." Jackson laughed. "He's a good guy."

"You've done right by him. Got him educated and given him a family. You're like a father to him."

"Oh please," Jackson griped. "Now you sound like Alex."

Kieran laughed but stopped when a scream filled the air.

They both turned toward the west, where the sound had come from.

"It looks like it's dinner time," Kieran observed.

"Yep," Jackson agreed. "Let's go."

They raced off toward what sounded like a scuffle. As they got closer, Kieran could almost hear the entire conversation. The woman begging for whoever had cornered her to just take her money and let her go. She had a son she needed to get home to.

Kieran made it into the alley just as one of the guys threw her down. She cried out as another, a tall skinny blond, stalked toward her.

"Please," she begged.

"Well, what do we have here?" Kieran asked

The woman gasped and started to cry harder as the blond kid and the dark-haired guy took up defensive stances.

"She's ours," the blond said. "Go find your own fun."

"Oh no," Jackson replied. "This looks like something we'll want a part of." He strolled forward and Kieran wasn't surprised when the younger guys backed off.

They were human and might not recognize them as being Walkers, but their build was much larger than the attackers'.

"Let me help you, ma'am," Jackson reached down and lifted the woman to her feet. "Now I want you to run as fast and far away from here as you can. Do you understand me?"

"Yes." She wiped her face. "Yes."

"Go now," Jackson ordered.

Kieran stalked forward, ignoring the woman and keeping his eyes on the two guys. They'd picked a good spot for their attempted assault. There was no way out of the alley.

"So you like to pick on women?" Kieran asked the blond.

"It was none of your business," Blondie replied.

"Maybe not," Kieran said. "But I made it mine." He lunged at the blond and had him off his feet in a matter of seconds. Beside him, he heard Jackson punch the dark-haired guy.

"Hey, man, it's cool," the blond told him. "We didn't mean any harm."

"And what would you have done to her if we hadn't come by?" Kieran asked.

"Nothing," Blondie said. "Really."

He was lying and they both knew it. Kieran slammed Blondie against the old brick building, twice. "What's your name?"

"What?"

"I asked what your name is," Kieran repeated. "And if you lie to me, I'll know."

"Du...Dustin," Blondie responded shakily.

Kieran reached around and pulled the wallet from Blondie's back pocket. He flipped it open. Dustin Evers. Kieran memorized his address.

"Now I know your name, face and address," Kieran told

him. "If you even think about doing something like this again, I will find you and you won't get off so easy next time."

Dustin nodded. "Promise!"

"Good," Kieran praised. "Not that you're going to get off too easy this time."

Dustin's eyes widened before Kieran threw him across the alley. Dustin hit the sidewalk and rolled. Kieran leapt after him and by the time Dustin stopped, he had his hand back around Dustin's thick neck.

"You'll learn your lesson," Kieran told him.

"Yes! Yes!" Dustin yelled.

Kieran drew his hand back and delivered three hard punches to the side of Dustin's face. Once he was unconscious, Kieran picked up Dustin's limp wrist and bit down.

The blood flooded his mouth and he swallowed. Immediately his body warmed. That was the danger when he drank. Not that he would lose control, but that he wouldn't stop, because there was never a time when he was as warm as when he drank blood.

He kept his eyes open and on Dustin. The kid might be a creep, but he wasn't going to die that night.

After half a dozen gulps of blood, Kieran dropped Dustin's wrist back down to the ground.

Not only would Dustin wake up with several bruises and possibly a fractured jaw, but he would be sick for the next several days from Kieran's bite. He straightened up and glanced to the side, where the dark-haired kid was braced against the wall. Jackson finished his phone call then turned to Kieran.

"A couple of my guys are going to come down here and wait until they wake up," Jackson told him. "Scare them a little more before taking them home."

"I usually just leave them."

"I figured," Jackson said. "But I don't want them back in this neighborhood. We both know what they would have done to that woman. She had a uniform on, cleaning outfit for one of the other hotels around here. She should be able to walk to and from work without being bothered."

Kieran just grinned. Jackson couldn't help but to try to save everyone. Even when Kieran had been giving up after living years in captivity, Jackson had managed to make him care again, make him want to survive.

"So how did it feel?" Kieran asked him.

Jackson grinned. "Better than I remembered."

With a laugh, they started out of the alley. Kieran would trust Jackson's guys to take care of the two humans and they had only a few hours before the sun would come up.

"We should get back to the hotel," Jackson commented.

Kieran paused at the mouth of the alley. The hair on the back of his neck stood up and the feeling of darkness surrounded him. "Jackson," he whispered.

"I sense it too." Jackson moved until they were back to back.

Kieran scanned the surrounding area but didn't pick up anyone or anything. "What is it?"

"I don't know," Jackson admitted.

The sudden cackle was loud and almost brought Kieran to his knees. He knew that sound.

"Well, well, well." Bradley stepped out of the shadows. He had his arm around the neck of the woman they'd saved earlier. "My two favorite pets together again."

Looking at the man who was responsible for their years of torment, Kieran felt like that scared eighteen-year-old kid again. He began to shake, but Jackson was there, pressing the back of his hand to Kieran's.

"Now, Kieran," Bradley said silkily. "I thought I taught you not to feed in public. Wasn't that how I found you the first time?"

Kieran refused to let his mind wander back into memories.

"Pretty ballsy, coming out here by yourself," Kieran taunted. "I also remember you being quite the coward. Never getting your own hands dirty."

Bradley snarled at him. "Am I supposed to fear you?" he asked Kieran. "I'm surprised you're not pissing yourself."

So was Kieran, but Bradley didn't need to know that. He snorted in response.

"Why don't you let the woman go and we'll talk this out, just the three of us," Jackson suggested.

Bradley glanced at the woman he held and blinked in surprise. Like he'd forgotten she was even there. Her quiet pleading wasn't doing anything to persuade him to release her. "This thing?" Bradley asked, shaking her roughly. "I couldn't care less about her. But it seems you still see yourself as a hero." Bradley laughed before he threw the woman down the street. With his shifter strength, she flew through the air before landing with a hard thud.

"What do you want?" Kieran asked.

Bradley turned his attention back to Kieran. "You, of course."

"I don't think so," Kieran snapped. "You must be even crazier than you used to be."

"Not even to save your friend's boy?" Bradley asked glancing between them. "He doesn't take to pain like you did. I don't think he'll make it another twenty-four hours."

"I'm going to kill you," Jackson spat.

"You'll try," Bradley said. "But, like all the others, you'll fail. Now if you don't mind, I'm trying to talk to Kieran. It's rude to interrupt."

Kieran couldn't believe this was happening. "And if I agree to go with you, you'll let Alex and the shifters go?" He had no intention of giving into this madman, but he wanted to know Bradley's plan.

"Wouldn't you rather I kept the shifters and let you play with them?" Bradley asked sweetly. "Oh no! That's right, you've taken a liking to a shifter. I could always bring her with you."

Kieran saw red, rage filling him. He took a step forward with his hands clenched. Jackson grabbed his shoulder and yanked him back.

Bradley let his amusement show by clapping.

"Oh my! What a reaction," Bradley taunted. "Maybe you've taken more than just a liking to the jaguar. That could prove very entertaining."

"You won't get your hands on her," Jackson declared.

"I could also take the wolf you like to hang out with," Bradley told him. "I've been watching you for a very long time. It seems you made yourself a little family. I would hate to break it up."

"You're messing with a whole lot more than just some terrified kid this time," Kieran warned.

"Oh, pish posh," Bradley waved his hand around. "The Organization? I've been outwitting them for years. You think Caspar is going to come to your rescue again? Trust me, he won't even make it here."

Cold dread traveled up Kieran's spine. "What did you do?"

Bradley's smiled was predatory. "Let's just say not everyone on his team is loyal to him. He'll be finding that out very shortly."

Kieran had had enough. He growled and crouched.

"Let's not fight," Bradley held up his hands. "Come with me and all your little friends will be safe. I can't say the same about Caspar, though. He's been a thorn in my side for way too long. He's the reason I lost you in the first place."

"Sure," Kieran said. "I'll come with you. I'll deliver your dead body to your men."

Kieran launched himself through the air and closed the distance between them. Bradley scrambled back and whistled.

Snarling, growling and snapping sounds came all around him. In the time Bradley had distracted them, he'd been able to move his shifters in close. Kieran couldn't worry about him though. He only had eyes for Bradley. He was going to tear out his throat.

Before Kieran could tackle Bradley like he had planned, a large weight knocked him out of the air. Kieran landed and rolled and was immediately back on his feet. In front of him was a huge black bear. The bear stood up on his hind legs and roared.

If Bradley didn't think he and Jackson could take care of six shifters, Kieran was going to have to believe the man *had* gotten crazier over time. Kieran darted forward and punched the bear in the stomach as hard as he could. The bear shifter tumbled away, only to be replaced by a tiger and coyote shifter. Kieran didn't waste any time going after them.

The shifters were good fighters, better than Kieran was used to, but still no match for a Walker. Once all his opponents were laid out, he turned and checked in on Jackson, who was laying the last of his adversaries flat.

Kieran turned back toward where Bradley had been, but he wasn't there any longer.

"Over here!"

He whirled around and saw Bradley two blocks away. He'd undressed and Kieran couldn't believe he was about to lose this fucker. He took off in a sprint, but before he'd even closed half the distance, Bradley had shifted.

Kieran leapt up and reached out as Bradley took flight, but there was no catching the eagle shifter.

"*Fuck!*" Kieran yelled out his frustration.

Chapter Seven

Kieran led the way into his suite and stopped short. Dakota and Remy were both sitting in the living room, staring at the door.

"Morning," Kieran greeted. He could tell from the looks on their faces that they'd been worried and were relieved to see them. The anger radiating from both their scents told a different story. *Damn, what did they know?*

Dakota stood and looked him up and down. "You okay?" she asked. Then she leaned in and sniffed him, actually sniffed him. Other than his clothes, he wouldn't smell like anything else. She nodded. Oh, fuck, she was checking for blood.

"Yeah, sure," he replied. "Fine."

She nodded again before spinning on her heel and stomping off.

"Dakota?" he called after her, but she didn't stop. Instead, after she'd crossed the threshold to the bedroom, she slammed the door once inside. Kieran turned to his partner. "What the hell?"

"What the hell?" Remy repeated. "What the hell? You find out Bradley is back in town and looking for you and you disappear?"

Oh, well, fuck. He hadn't counted on anyone knowing that yet. "How'd you know?"

"Seriously!" Remy yelled as he threw up his hands. "I was CC'd on the fucking email. Do you really think Caspar would have only sent it to you? Didn't you see the others?"

No, he hadn't, but he'd been tired and hungry.

"So your girlfriend and I have been sitting here for over

an hour waiting for you," Remy finished.

"Oh," Kieran said lamely.

"What the fuck, man!" Remy shoved his shoulder as he passed.

"What are you doing?" Kieran asked. He didn't want Remy leaving, out on the streets alone. Bradley had already made a threat against him.

"I'm ordering some breakfast for us all," Remy replied angrily.

Kieran glanced at Jackson and saw him staring back. They hadn't quite figured out what to do about telling the others of their run-in with Bradley. They needed to get a warning out to Caspar if possible. Kieran had already tried Caspar's cell phone, but it kept going to voicemail.

Jackson gave him a small nod. Looked like they were going to have to come clean about everything.

"Let me go talk to Dakota," Kieran told Remy. "After you order us some breakfast, Jackson will fill you in."

"Fine." Remy waved him off.

At least his partner's scent had lessened to a more manageable irritated one. He'd probably still have to hear about it later from Remy, but he wanted to handle only one fight at a time.

Kieran shuffled his feet on the way to the bedroom. He'd heard the shower turn on already and knew Dakota was in the bathroom and he really wanted to avoid this confrontation.

"Stop acting like a baby," Remy hollered at him.

Kieran flipped him off before he turned the knob on the bedroom door. At least it wasn't locked. He strolled into the bedroom as the shower turned off.

Instead of meeting her in the bathroom, he walked over to the bed and sat down.

Dakota came out of the bathroom with a towel wrapped around her body and another in her hand with which she was drying her hair.

"I'm sorry," he told her.

"Did you feed?" she asked as she tossed one of her towels onto the chair.

"I did," he answered. She didn't say anything else as she began to dress. Kieran waited until she'd outfitted herself in dark jeans and a black t-shirt and was pulling on her boots before he stood and went to her. "I'm sorry."

"I heard you."

"Look at me." He grabbed her chin and forced her to comply. "Are you going to tell me why you're mad?"

"Would you like a list?"

"Uh." Kieran just wasn't fucking sure what the right answer was.

"You went out to hunt by yourself," Dakota began, holding up one finger. "Mitch showed me the video of you leaving the hotel. You walked right past Jackson and didn't even notice him. If he hadn't followed you, would you have been in trouble?"

Kieran sighed.

"That's what I thought," Dakota continued and put up a second finger. "And I haven't forgotten the fact that you left the hotel minutes after finding out Bradley was in town and possibly after you."

"Yes," he admitted.

"So did you see him?"

"Yes."

"And you're okay?"

"I am," Kieran assured her. "I wasn't thinking."

"That's pretty obvious," she deadpanned.

"Are you going to be mad at me all day?" Kieran asked, frustrated. "I fucked up, but I refuse to grovel." He knew he'd messed up even before she jerked away. Damn, this was not going the way he wanted. He'd apologized and Dakota just needed to let it go. Still, he could have phrased it better.

"Grovel?" she repeated. "Is that what you think I want?" Instead of yelling, her voice dropped and actually gave him a chill.

"I don't know what you want," he yelled because he couldn't help himself. He could actually feel Dakota putting up a wall between them and it hurt. Instead of trying to reassure her, he lashed out.

"I want you to stop finding excuses for pushing me away," she told him quietly.

"I don't."

She whirled around and paced to the window. With her back to him Kieran was barely able to hang on to his control. He wanted her to look at him like she used to. With wonder and passion.

"It doesn't matter."

He took a step forward, but she was already moving to the side and across the room.

"We need to hurry up and get ready for the operation this morning," she said.

Before Kieran could respond, she had the door open and was striding away. He could hear her talking to Remy and Jackson. He sat back down on the mattress and put his head in his hands. What in the hell was happening? It'd been so right between them the night before and now everything was twisted around. He knew she was worried about him, but her behavior was off.

He pushed himself up off the bed as someone knocked on the front door. He sighed. Okay, he couldn't have it out with Dakota at that moment, but they were going to talk this through. Damon's voice carried to him and he had to fight his instincts to attack. His fangs dropped and his heart sped up. Kieran clenched his fists until he was calm again, then walked out of the bedroom to join the others. He spotted Damon bent over and whispering in Dakota's ear.

Kieran roared and launched himself across the room.

"*Shit!*" Remy yelled as Damon grabbed Dakota and threw her to the floor.

Kieran didn't knock into Damon, though. Jackson was there and Kieran was slamming into his body.

"No!" Kieran screamed as he and Jackson rolled.

Hands grabbed him and Kieran fought with everything he had. No! Not again, they weren't going to take him again.

The scent of wolf shifters was strong. There was more than one and Kieran couldn't seem to get a good look around him. His eyes wouldn't focus and he couldn't catch his breath. For some reason his strength wasn't at normal level. Had they already gotten him? Had he tried to escape like he'd done once before?

What day was it? He wasn't cold like normal so maybe they were trying a different type of experiment. They loved to mess with his head. He felt carpet under his arms, but that didn't make sense. The concrete was always so hard and cold. Kieran was rolled over onto his stomach with his arms jerked back.

He screamed and kicked but managed to catch one of his attackers. The pressure at the back of his neck didn't hurt, which confused him. They always hurt him.

Kieran closed his eyes to try to concentrate better, but his mind wouldn't stop spinning. He shifted enough to get his knees under him and pushed up with a roar. Whoever was on his back went flying off and Kieran scrambled to his knees before making it to his feet.

"Stay away!" he ordered and swung at the figure moving closer. What the fuck had they done to his eyes? He couldn't see right!

"Kieran."

He knew that voice. Or at least he thought he did. No, they used recordings. They'd tricked him before. When they'd played Jack begging over and over. This was just another trick.

"Kieran, it's okay. Open your eyes."

He shook his head. He had his eyes open, didn't he?

"Love."

His face was cupped. Comfort? Caring? He didn't understand. "It's me. Open your eyes."

Kieran complied and blinked right before lips covered his. Dakota was blurry, but he knew her taste and the feel of her. He wrapped his arms around her back and yanked her closer.

When they parted, he blinked at her in confusion. "What happened?"

Remy and Damon were helping each other up while Jackson remained on his knees.

"I think you had some sort of flashback," Dakota told him.

"Here? Now?" Kieran questioned.

"Did you know you were fighting us? Did you know where you were?" Dakota asked.

"No," Kieran confessed. "I thought I was back…there."

"What's the last thing you remember before you went back there?" Dakota queried.

Kieran glanced around and his gaze landed on Damon. He'd been jealous of the Alpha being close to Dakota. "Just coming into the room and seeing Damon."

Dakota followed to where the Alpha was now picking up some of the broken plates from their table. "Did you remember something?" she whispered.

"No. Just the scent of the wolf shifters. I'm used to Remy, but having another in here confused me for a minute."

She nodded. "I understand. I want to rub and scratch up against everything in this room every time Remy leaves."

Kieran frowned. "Why haven't you ever told me?"

"It's no big deal," she said with a shrug. "I've always had to share my space, so I'm used to it."

He didn't want that for her, though. She'd gone from training campuses to staying in the Organization's lodgings. This was the first time Dakota had actually been able to completely relax and call her residence a home. Maybe they needed to think about something more permanent. He'd miss the little extra comforts the hotel offered, but it was more important Dakota had her first real home.

Maybe he'd talk to Jackson about finding them an apartment or condo. He'd also see what he could do about the scents others brought in.

"Are you listening to me?" Dakota gripped his shoulder.

"Sorry." He shook his thoughts away. "I guess tonight affected me more than I thought."

"It's okay," she told him. "It's going to be okay."

Kieran grasped the back of her neck and pulled her in

until their foreheads touched. "Tell me we'll get through this." He needed to hear the words. He would know if she was lying.

"Yes," she told him. "Couples fight. It doesn't mean I stop having feelings for you. Or I'd pick another shifter over you."

Her knowing smile made him wince.

"This is going to be over soon. Bradley and his people will pay for what they did to you and you'll go back to playing pranks on poor Organization agents," she said.

He relaxed then took a step back. "Sorry," he told the others.

"No problem." Remy waved his hand. "I missed my morning workout anyway."

Jackson gave his arm a squeeze as he passed while Damon simply nodded. Kieran didn't like being out of control and he was going to end this torment once and for all. He had his lover, best friend and oldest friend at his back, as well as an Alpha wolf and trained agents. Bradley wouldn't get away this time. Kieran was going to make him pay.

Dakota smiled at him before taking his hand and leading him to the table. "Let's fuel up. We've got a big day ahead of us."

"So I take it we're not going to wait like Caspar asked?" Remy questioned.

"No," Kieran replied. "I want this over with before he arrives. He's spent enough time chasing this bastard."

* * * *

Kieran couldn't shake the feeling that he was close to finding Bradley. Excitement coursed through him, making it hard for him to keep his fangs inside, and he knew his eyes were glowing.

The entire group had met up a few miles away from where they believed Bradley and his crew were holding Alex and the shifters.

"You sure he doesn't suspect we know where he is?" Remy asked.

"He wouldn't have let us go last night," Kieran assured him. "He still thinks I'm afraid of him. He tried to use that against me."

"We'll be sure to use that against him," Jackson said.

This was it. After so many years of living in fear, he was going to end this for everyone. Not only him and Jackson, but anyone who could be a future target.

"Are we ready?" Dakota asked.

Kieran looked around him. This was an odd bunch working together. Walkers, Organization agents and local wolf shifters.

"We have to plan," Kieran said. "Let's split up and finish this."

Dakota was the first one to step out of the circle they'd made. She began lifting her shirt over her head so she could shift. Kieran followed, not only blocking her from view, but also so he could speak to her.

As she crouched, he bent down above her. "No matter what happens, you get out safe. Promise me even if you have to leave me behind, you won't get captured."

Her hazel gaze met his. "I promise."

He kissed her forehead and waited until she shifted. It appeared seamless. One minute she was a human, the next a jaguar. He petted her head. "Go stretch your legs while I talk to Remy."

She licked him with her rough tongue before striding off.

Kieran turned to where his partner had already taken off his clothes. He hurried over before Remy could transform.

"What is it?" Remy asked when Kieran reached him.

"I need you to promise me something," Kieran whispered. This was definitely not a conversation he wanted anyone else to hear.

"Anything, you know that," Remy replied instantly.

"If they get me, I need you to kill me. Don't let me end up in their hands again."

"I…" Remy shook his head. "What?"

Kieran grabbed his arm. "I can't go through the torture again. Kill me before they can get me."

"You're not easy to kill," Remy reminded him.

"But you know how," Kieran said. It was one of the first lessons taught in the Organization. Walkers were not an enemy they came across often and it was easier for another Walker to end them, but there were ways.

Remy bit his lip but eventually nodded. "I promise I'll do whatever I have to."

That was good enough for him. Remy would keep his word. The bond they'd formed would insist on it.

"Thank you," Kieran murmured.

"But when we get out of this, we're going to have a serious discussion about your suicidal tendencies," Remy promised.

Kieran grinned. "Whatever you want."

Remy began his transformation, so Kieran went back to Jackson and the other Walkers. "We go in silent," he said, joining them. "Bradley might not be expecting us, but he's going to have guards and some sort of warning system."

"We're faster than the shifters, so we'll get in first," Jackson stated.

"The shifters' priority is to get Alex and the others out," Kieran said.

"And ours?" Jackson asked.

"Have your men help our shifters," Kieran ordered. "You and I are going to find Bradley. He's not escaping this time."

"Deal." Jackson gripped his shoulder. "They're ready."

The track wasn't going to take long. Kieran had tried to keep the human Organization agents out of the caves, but they'd insisted on coming along, using the argument that they were probably the safest. Kieran couldn't dispute that fact, but they were also the most vulnerable. Bradley would have no issue killing them.

They traveled in a straight line, covering the distance quickly. The shifters were keeping pace with them easily enough, but he could hear the labored breathing of the humans. However they were almost to the opening. Kieran rushed ahead, putting himself in front of Damon. Even if the Alpha knew the area better, Kieran wasn't letting anyone cross into the hellish nightmare he knew would be ahead of them.

There were no sounds around them. The public hiking areas were miles away from where they were. It was smart of Bradley to have set up shop here, if this was indeed where the operation was. And Kieran was almost certain they'd found the right spot.

The closer they got to the cave entrance, the more the entire area seemed entrenched in evil.

It wasn't a scent, but instead a feeling.

Kieran paused when the opening came into view. This was it. He took a deep breath before he glanced over his shoulder. Everyone seemed focused and ready. He took a moment to look at each of them. The Walkers' eyes were glowing and their fangs on display. The shifters were poised and ready to fight. Even the humans appeared determined.

He nodded once then looked back at the cave.

He ran.

The scenery didn't even register to him as he sped past. All his attention was on the destination. He crossed over the threshold and knew instantly this was where the first guards were stationed.

He had the element of surprise on his side, though. Kieran slid on his knees past the two shifter security personnel. He brought up his arm and grabbed the closest one as the rest of his group followed him in.

Kieran threw the shifter, a lion, against the wall as hard as he could. The resounding smack echoed around the small area. There was a gasp before the sound came of another body hitting the ground. Kieran rose and saw Dean checking the pulse of the guard one of the others had taken out.

"He's alive," Dean said. "I'll get them cuffed and keep

them here. Go ahead."

Kieran nodded before he took off again. The tunnel was crudely made but was big enough for him to stand in, so that made running easier. He hadn't gotten more than a couple of yards before he slid to a stop. He felt the others at his back as well, even though none of them made a sound.

"There," he whispered and pointed up at the camera they were just out of view of.

"What do we do?" Dakota's lips were right by his ear.

He turned toward her surprised. He hadn't heard her or anyone else shift back. "I can probably get past without it catching sight of me. All the Walkers can."

"What about the rest of us?"

"We can try to find the surveillance room and take out the guards in there and get the cameras offline," he suggested.

"You mean go alone?"

"I'll be with him." Jackson joined them.

"Ten minutes," she told him. "I'm going down that hall in ten minutes whether those cameras are on or not."

"Okay." He grabbed Jackson. "Move as fast as you ever have in your life."

"Right behind you," Jackson said before motioning to the other Walkers.

It was a chance, but with his full strength, Kieran was certain he could move fast enough that his image would not be caught. He closed his eyes before he raced down the hall.

The rush he got was incredible. He'd never experienced anything like it before. He wanted to roar, to call out to his prey. It was different but felt so right.

There was a turn at the end of the first section. Kieran backed up against the wall and held up his hand so the others wouldn't move. He listened, but it took a few moments before he caught the two different footsteps and soft voices.

He held up two fingers, letting Jackson and his men know there were two guards ahead. Jackson patted his shoulder twice and Kieran went into action. He was halfway to the bear shifter before he was spotted, but it was too late. A few quick jabs and they were out.

Power rolled through him.

"Cuff their wrists and put them in the corner. They'll be unconscious long enough for the shifters to catch up," Jackson told him.

"Okay." He accepted the plastic ties and secured the shifters.

"We still need to hurry," Jackson said as Kieran finished.

Kieran nodded. They were already through three makeshift halls and he still didn't think they were close to the center. However long Bradley had been operating out of the mountain, it was obvious he'd put a lot of time and energy into the space. Just like he'd done with Mount Fauna.

"Follow me," Kieran said.

He searched the walls and ceiling for more cameras and every time he spotted one he signaled behind him then sped past it. He knew it wouldn't be much longer before Dakota and the shifters followed, so they needed to find the security area. Which should have been easy enough until they got to a place where there were two tunnels.

"Left," Kieran said. "I can't hear anything, but I just have a feeling."

"Me too," Jackson agreed. "But we still need to check both. I'll go with you and my men will take the right."

"The shifters won't know which way to go," Kieran reminded him. Without them having a scent, it would be hard for Dakota to follow.

"We have to take the chance. We don't have much time before they'll be on their way, and we need those cameras off or Bradley will know we're here," Jackson stated.

"If they don't already," Kieran commented.

"I don't think so." Jackson held up an earpiece. "There's no chatter yet."

Kieran breathed a sigh of relief. *This might actually work.*

"To the left then." He strolled a little deeper into their passageway while Jackson went over the plan with his men.

Once Jackson was with him again, Kieran turned to his old friend.

"I can't believe we're here again."

"It's time for our revenge," Jackson replied.

"Just be safe," Kieran said.

"About that." Jackson gripped his arm. "I heard what you made Remy promise. I need the same from you."

"No," Kieran said automatically.

"I won't make it. I can't go through this again."

"I do know," Kieran said. "I won't let them take you alive."

"Thank you," Jackson replied.

Kieran glanced at his watch. "We only have four minutes."

"So let's run," Jackson said before he sprinted off.

He grinned as he followed Jackson deeper into the mountain. The adrenaline was so strong it seemed like his hearing was increasing. Finally, he could hear others walking around, talking and even moaning. He'd been right. They were headed to the correct location.

Light began to bleed through. They crept the rest of the way to the opening and peered out.

The room that had been built was a large space with the walls forming a circle that also showed the openings of four additional tunnels. Five guards stood around the area, laughing and talking.

Kieran backed up, pulling Jackson with him. "Now what?"

"We can take them."

"There're cameras all over that room."

"So we'll lose the element of surprise."

"We could wait for the others."

"No," Jackson answered. "We're too close."

Kieran nodded. "They'll send more in as soon as they spot us."

"Dakota and the others will be here soon. Let's clear the

way."

"On the count of three," Kieran ordered.

Together they moved to the mouth of the gap. Kieran held up his fist then began the countdown. Once three fingers were in the air, they leapt out of their hiding place and attacked.

Roaring filled the small space, but Kieran ignored the distraction. Instead he concentrated on each move. He was so focused he could see each strike and kick as if he was watching from afar. He didn't understand what was happening with his senses and powers, but Kieran was going to use them to his advantage.

He took out three before he heard Dakota's call.

She was coming.

"Finish this off," Kieran yelled to Jackson as he leapt to his feet. He darted through the opening in front of him, his instincts pushing him on. His vision narrowed until he could only see a small pinprick ahead.

The lab.

The scent of blood, bile, fear and agony were overpowering, but Kieran didn't slow down. He knew it was just up ahead. He could taste the death in his mouth.

He slid to a stop at the steel door. It was so familiar to him. Just like the one at Mount Fauna. He put his hand on the knob, forcing himself to continue. He yelped and jerked back as electricity scorched him.

Fuck! He'd forgotten they did that. The guards had worn rubber gloves and always let the door open from the inside. They knocked. Three times.

Kieran stepped back then raised his hand to the door and knocked, three times.

"Who is that?" Someone asked.

"One of the shifters that is scheduled," another answered.

The second voice sent a shiver of chill down his spine. He knew that voice. It'd been haunting him for years. Kieran took a deep breath and knocked again, three times.

"Coming!" someone who had to be the guard yelled.

Kieran moved to the side of the door and waited. As soon as the door opened, he slammed his fist into the opening and landed a hard punch to the guard's face. He used all his strength and the guard went flying back.

"*What?*" the doctor hollered.

Kieran followed the guard in and slammed the door behind him. He turned and faced the hyena shifter. His heart was pounding, but Kieran didn't know whether it was fear or excitement. He'd dreamed of this moment for so long. "Hello, Doc."

The asshole actually smiled at him. "Kieran, my pet."

The response threw him off, but he wouldn't let the doc see it. He glanced over to the guard and saw him lying with his head angled wrong. Oops, looked like he'd broken the guy's neck. He gave his attention back to the psychotic in front of him. The last time that Kieran had seen him, Kieran had been desperately clinging to life. As many times as he'd prayed to die and just have his pain end, Kieran was a fighter.

"You don't look surprised to see me, Doc," Kieran said. He rolled his shoulders back and made sure he was at his full height. The years with the Organization had made him fit and he was proud to stand strong in front of his biggest nightmare.

"Because I'm not," the madman responded with a smirk. "I told Bradley it was a mistake to continue my research here after you came to town."

Kieran ignored the mention of Bradley for the moment. This was about him and the man who'd grinned and laughed as he'd tormented Kieran. "How long have you been here?" Kieran questioned. He wanted to believe that the fucking experiments hadn't continued the entire time Kieran had been free. His stomach rolled just at the thought.

"Since I had to leave you behind. We'd already begun work on this new establishment. You were going to be our first patient, but the Organization got too close."

Kieran snorted. "Establishment? It's not exactly five star

here."

The doctor sighed deeply. "I know. I've had to make sacrifices for the cause."

"The cause?" Kieran repeated in disgust. It'd been a few years, but it was obvious the doctor had seriously lost his mind.

"To make the greatest supernatural creation ever."

"Why would you want to do that?"

The doc shook his head as he walked over to a stool. He sat before spinning around to face Kieran.

"Everlasting life, of course," Doc answered.

"There is no such thing."

"Not yet," Doc agreed. "But if we combine the best genes of the shifters and your kind, we might be able to create something that can come close."

"We don't need shifter genes. We can already do all that. That's what makes my kind special." Kieran made sure his tone held the right amount of mockery.

"Except for the fact that most of you go crazy and end up homicidal."

"Except that," Kieran admitted dismissively.

The doctor waved his finger at him. "But you're different. Even after everything that was done to you, somehow you never allowed the darkness in."

Kieran laughed. "Guess you haven't been paying attention."

"Oh, you went a little crazy," Doc said. "But you also formed bonds with your partner. A wolf shifter."

"And?"

"And," Doc continued, "you fell in love."

Kieran stiffened even though he really tried not to.

"Don't worry. I have a plan for the two of you. It doesn't include her joining my little family yet."

"What plan?"

"That, I'm not going to tell you. Not quite yet."

"Then I might as well kill you," Kieran said.

"You won't kill me," Doc said.

Kieran let his fangs drop. It was time to use his rage. He wanted to rub his hands together and laugh, but that was over the top even for him. "Oh yeah, I think I will."

"You'll never get the answer you need."

"I don't need anything from you," Kieran said. He didn't know what the doctor was trying to play at, but the shifter did love his games. "In fact" — Kieran crept closer — "I'm really going to enjoy this."

Kieran grabbed the doctor by the lapels of his coat, lifted him up and dangled him off the ground. His glowing eyes warned the doc he was about to lose some blood. Hell, even his mouth watered.

"Do it!" Doc ordered. "Bite me, Kieran."

"Gladly." Kieran bent forward.

"*Don't!*" Dakota yelled as she rushed in.

Kieran snarled but turned his head to Dakota.

"It's what he wants," she said. "And if it's what he wants then you shouldn't do it."

Chapter Eight

Dakota hoped like hell Kieran listened to her, because she'd heard the doctor tell Kieran to bite him, and that wasn't right. She couldn't let this man hurt her lover ever again. He was trying to fuck with Kieran's mind and that was unacceptable. If she hadn't promised to bring in as many alive as she could, she'd slash his throat. Of course, she would have to shift back into her jaguar form.

"Kieran, don't do it."

His eyes were still glowing, but it wasn't the same blue she'd seen before. Red bled through. He wouldn't even be aware.

"You have to stop."

"I want him dead."

"I know," she answered. "But think."

He blinked and his eyes went back to normal.

"Don't listen to her," Doc said. "She's just jealous."

"What?" she and Kieran said at the same time.

"See?" she pointed out. "Something's off."

Kieran lowered the doctor and Dakota walked closer to him. She pulled out a pair of cuffs and secured him before drawing her fist back and hitting him as hard as she could. Kieran let the doctor drop to the ground.

"That was my job," he bitched. "And you're naked."

Dakota laughed. "You can have the next one." She stepped over the doctor and cupped Kieran's face. "It was the right thing to do. There are too many unanswered questions. And I'll shift back to my jaguar in a minute."

"I want in on his interrogation," Kieran demanded.

Dakota sighed. The Organization had their own team

of interrogators who were trained to be the absolute best at extracting information. Kieran would be entering a dangerous situation. Walkers excelled at interrogation, but they didn't last long in the position. They already suffered the dangerous affliction of going insane and attacking innocents. Very few managed to hang on to their humanity like Kieran. Dakota believed in her lover, but she still worried how any questioning of his enemies would affect him.

"I'm not asking," Kieran said.

"Fine," Dakota replied. "We still haven't found Alex or the shifters."

"I'm not leaving him." Kieran waved his hand at the doctor.

"I'll stay with him." Gabe stepped into the room.

Kieran glanced over at the bear shifter.

"I trust him," Dakota told her lover. "He's my partner."

"I won't let him out of my sight. I swear to you," Gabe said.

When Kieran still hesitated, Dakota gripped his hand. "We still need to get Bradley too."

She saw that connect with him so she pushed more. "Gabe will stay in this room with the doctor. I need you with me."

Kieran turned to Gabe. "He'll mess with your mind. Don't believe anything he says."

Gabe grinned then walked over to a cabinet. He sorted through a cabinet of some bottles before he held one up. "Got it." He picked up a syringe next. "This will keep him out for hours. He won't get a chance to mess with my head."

"Perfect," Kieran responded.

Dakota nodded at her partner before grabbing Kieran's wrist and yanking him out of the door. "There's more tunnels to search."

They raced back toward the center room that gave access to the other tunnels.

"Which one?" Dakota asked.

Kieran looked frantically around. "I don't know. I don't

know."

"You have to decide." His instincts had been spot on so far. "Which one?"

"There's two. I feel I need to be in two places at once. Damn it!"

Shit, that meant they were going to have to split up again. She really didn't want to do that. "Which two?"

"This one." Kieran pointed. "And that one."

"Fine." She pushed Kieran toward the closest opening. "You go that way and I'll take this one."

"Wait!" Kieran cried.

Dakota spun back around. "What?"

"Be careful," he told her.

"Always." She winked at him. She dropped to her knees and called forward her animal. It took a little longer than usual, but eventually she was her large cat again. It always took a toll on her body to shift back and forth, but she'd had to return to human form when she'd heard the doctor tell Kieran he had a plan for them.

She would be paying for it later, but she'd had to shift.

Now she was back on all four paws, she sprinted down the tunnel. Their group had split up, so she was sure one of her team was already down this way, but that didn't mean she didn't need to be careful.

As she ran, she listened for any sound, but it was hard to concentrate. The scents around her lowered all her other senses. She heard a scream and sped up. Dakota reached the gap in the cave faster than she realized. She tried to slow down, but her claws slipped on the smoothed-out ground and she flew out into the hall.

She smacked the opposite wall with a thud.

"Ouch, that sounded like it hurt."

Dakota rolled onto her paws and looked up. Damon stood above her, naked and grinning. She swiped her paw at him to get him to back off.

"Okay, little cat," Damon said. "I can smell my pack members close by."

So could she, along with other species of shifters. They'd found the rescued shifters. She could also smell death. They weren't going to be bringing everyone back alive.

Screaming split the air.

"Come on!" Damon roared before he started to shift.

Dakota leapt over him before she hurried toward the sound. When she reached the steel door, she rammed it, but it barely moved.

"Here, let me."

She looked up and saw one of Jackson's Walkers standing beside Damon. Dakota moved over and the Walker grabbed the handle and pulled. There was a groan of metal before the steel began to bend.

Finally, the door came off the hinges and the Walker tossed it aside. Cages lined an entire room. The scent of shifters and death was so strong her eyes began to water.

She stepped inside, but the Walker placed his hand on her back.

"Be careful," he said. "We don't know if all the shifters in here are innocent."

Dakota paused before shaking her body. If she could get past the horrid smells inside, she could use her senses to find the injured and scared. She relaxed her body before taking another step. The first two cages were empty, but the third held a female cougar naked in human form. Dakota pressed her nose up to the cage. The female shifter started to shake and cry.

Dakota called forward her human form.

"It's okay," she told the young girl. "We're here to save you."

"G...gggooooo away," the cougar sobbed. "Thhhhhey'lll hurt you."

"No," Dakota assured her. "They won't hurt you anymore. We're getting you out of here."

She yanked on the door, but it didn't move. What the hell? She tried again. "What are these things made of?" she asked.

"I don't know," Damon said coming up behind her. "Let's try together."

Feet braced shoulder-width apart, she gripped one bar while Damon took another. They started to pull. It took all her strength, but finally they were able to bend the cage enough for Dakota to get through.

"We're not going to be able to do that for all of them," Dakota told Damon.

"You're right," he agreed. "I'll see if I can find someone who knows the codes." He cracked his knuckles. "This might be fun."

Dakota shook her head and crouched at the gap they'd made. "Stay here, we're going to get the others out."

The woman just stared blankly back at her.

"Okay," Dakota said and stood. She strolled down the line of cages, glancing at both sides. It worried her that many of them were unoccupied. Did that mean the others were already dead? Or were they somewhere in this maze of tunnels?

"*Alex?*" Dakota stepped up to the last cage. The Walker was sprawled on his back. "*Alex!*"

"They just brought him back. He'll be out for a while."

She looked over at the last cell and the young man who'd crawled forward and spoken.

"I don't think they hurt him as much as they did the first time," he told her.

"Hi," she said. "I'm Dakota." She sniffed and the strong odor of wolf shifter assaulted her. "Are you Max?"

"You know who I am?" he asked, surprised.

"We've been looking for you. Your Alpha is with us."

"Damon came?" Max curled his fingers around the bars. "He really came?"

"Of course he did. He went to find someone who knows the code to the doors."

"Five, one, one, three," Max said.

Dakota pressed the numbers into Max's keypad and the door clicked open. "Oh my god, Max! That's great. Is it the same for all the cells?"

Max nodded. "Alex told me the code. He said I would need to know it to get out."

Dakota threw the door open the rest of the way and went over to Max to help him to his feet. "Can you stand?"

"I think so." Max climbed to his feet but lurched forward. Dakota caught him.

"Come on. You need to help me with Alex."

"Yeah," Max replied. "I want to help him."

Even with Max's full mass, Dakota had no problem holding him up. The poor kid barely weighed anything at all. She lifted him up with her arm around his waist.

Once they stood back in front of Alex's cage and she punched in the same code, Alex's door opened. She glanced down the cages to where the Walker was still trying to pry the bars of one open.

"Five, one, one, three," she called to him. "That's the code."

"Okay," he yelled back. "I'll get them all open and we'll start taking them out."

"Thanks." She turned her attention back to Alex. She sat Max down on Alex's right side before moving to the left.

She checked his pulse, thankful Walkers actually had one. He was still alive, so that was good, but he'd been beaten savagely. There was blood all over his mouth and she pried his lips apart.

"They yanked his fangs."

She peered up at Damon.

"From what Jackson told me it was one of their favorite tricks. To yank out the Walkers' fangs," Damon told her.

Dakota knew that from Kieran, but she'd never really understood what had happened. There were giant holes in his gums. If this had happened to Kieran over and over... she couldn't imagine the pain.

He'd even told her the doctor had laughed and laughed as he'd done it. Shit, she should have let Kieran kill the fucking guy. Then no one would ever feel the agony these people had.

"Alpha?"

Max's voice drew her thoughts back to the present.

"It's okay." Damon dropped down beside his pack member. "I got you now." He gathered the younger wolf into his arms as Max began to sob. "You're safe."

"They told me you wouldn't come," Max said. "That you didn't care about us, me, any of us. That you were going to let me die here."

"Never." Damon rocked his wolf. "I would never leave you to suffer."

The heartwarming moment brought tears to Dakota's eyes. The tough Alpha comforting a member of his pack. Wasn't that what they were all looking for? Someone to care for them. Someone to care what would happen to him.

For so long she'd given everything to the Organization, but then she'd found Kieran. Now she had other priorities. Ones that put everything she believed in at risk. Instead of wanting to take the doctor and Bradley into custody, she wished she could just end them.

Alex groaned and Dakota leaned over him.

"Can you hear me, Alex?" Dakota said gently. "It's Dakota, we found you."

"Jackson?"

"He's here."

"They want him and Kieran again," Alex whispered.

"I know. Can you open your eyes?"

Alex blinked his eyes and when he did open them, they were glowing. "It hurts."

"Let's get you out of here," Dakota said.

"Can you take Max?" Damon said. "I'll carry him."

The Alpha was stronger than her. Damon stood with Max and she maneuvered herself to brace him. Damon bent and lifted Alex.

"Jackson," Alex muttered. "Where is Jackson?"

"We'll find him for you. He went down one of the other tunnels," Dakota said.

"Bradley," Alex managed before going into a coughing fit. "Bradley wants them."

She didn't know why he kept repeating himself, but she needed to get him out and see what she could do about getting him blood. That would be the quickest way to get him feeling better and hopefully making better sense.

"Lead the way," Damon told her.

Dakota helped steady Max and they stumbled out of the cell. They shuffled down the lines of cages with Damon carrying Alex, and Alex mumbling about Jackson, Kieran and Bradley the entire time.

The Walker was opening cells, telling the scared shifters someone would be right there to help them out. It didn't look like he was getting much of a response from any of the injured shifters.

As they reached the one cage she and Damon had gotten open, she was surprised to see the cougar gone.

"Hey!" she called to the Walker. "Did someone help the girl out of here?"

"Not yet," he answered. "Backup is on the way. No one's left yet."

"What is it?" Damon asked behind her.

"The female cougar," Dakota said. "She's gone."

"Maybe she got out on her own?"

"She was so scared. She didn't believe she was being rescued."

"With the opening, maybe she realized she was actually free."

Dakota shook her head. She'd find the young cougar and put her mind at ease once they got Max and Alex out.

"Where's Jackson?" Alex asked.

That was another good question. Where were Kieran and Jackson?

Dakota started to respond when two men stepped in front of her. Shifters, and since they were dressed and carrying weapons, she could not mistake them for victims. She glanced over her shoulder at Damon.

"You really don't want to get in our way," Damon told the guards.

Max stiffened. Dakota was getting a really bad feeling about these two.

"You think we're just going to let you walk out of here with them?" the biggest one asked. He was a grizzly shifter and Dakota hoped she didn't have to fight him. The cheetah shifter next to him wouldn't be a problem.

"Yes, we do."

Before either man could turn around or look at the Walker that had come up behind them, he'd knocked them all out.

"Fuckers," Max hissed. "They loved to torture us."

She might have moved a little slower than normal so Max could kick both downed shifters in the face, but Damon didn't comment and it appeared Alex had passed out again.

"I've been wanting to do that for a while," Max told her.

They stepped out of the hellhole and saw another bear shifter standing there. He was dressed like the other guards, but he was so young. He was staring at the big grizzly shifter on the ground.

The Walker crept up to the kid, who looked terrified. Dakota remembered when Kieran and Remy had been attacked at the tunnels. Kieran had told her about the young bear shifter and how he hadn't seemed like he'd wanted to be involved. If this was the same kid, she could easily see Kieran had been right.

"Wait! Stop!" The kid held his hands up before the Walker even reached him. "I didn't want to do any of it."

The Walker gripped the kid by the shoulder. "You related to him?"

"Yes," the young shifter replied quietly. "He's my older brother."

"Is that where you got all these?" The Walker turned the kid's face and Dakota saw huge dark bruises.

He nodded. "I didn't want to do it," the kid repeated.

"Okay, why don't you show me where the surveillance room is?" the Walker said.

"It's this way."

Over the young shifter's head, the Walker nodded at Dakota. She really need to pay better attention to Jackson's men. For the life of her, she couldn't think of the guy's name. She smiled, showing she appreciated the gentle hand with the kid. A lot of people had been hurt during this operation and it seemed not everyone was involved because they wanted to be.

She'd have to check on the kid once they returned to the office. If there was a story with his family, Dakota would find it out. She might have Dean dig a little for her.

* * * *

Kieran glanced over at Jackson, who nodded back at him. They'd found the offices and tracked Bradley's scent to the last one. The floor was littered with half a dozen guards, but Kieran was pretty sure they weren't dead. Well, almost sure, anyway.

He could hear movement behind the closed door. Kieran knocked three times.

"Give me a minute!" Bradley yelled. "I'm almost ready."

It was obvious Bradley didn't know who was at his door. He probably thought it was the guards waiting to get him out of there. With the lack of communication and no alarm sounding, Kieran was a little embarrassed it had taken them this long to capture Bradley. Jeez, the place should be full of guards and have a better security system. It didn't even seem to matter whether or not the security cameras were taken care of. Although he was going to make sure the equipment and tapes got sent to him at the office. He wanted to know everyone who'd been involved.

"He doesn't leave this cave," Jackson told him. "It's the perfect place for his dead body."

Kieran nodded then backed up. He ran at the door and raised his foot, kicking the metal barrier off the hinges and making it fly into the room. Jackson moved fast and by the time Kieran was in the room, Jackson had Bradley pinned up against the wall.

"Hello, Bradley," Jackson said, laughing. "Not expecting us?"

Bradley appeared so surprised he wasn't even fighting back. He had blood running down his temple and Kieran licked his lips. He wouldn't mind tasting the eagle shifter's blood. "I want to bite him."

"Go ahead," Jackson said. "He's not going anywhere."

Kieran stepped forward but Bradley turned his head and smiled at him. "Yes, Kieran, go ahead and take a bite."

That made him stop. Why wasn't the doctor or Bradley afraid of him? It didn't make sense. Unless they'd done something to him he couldn't remember? Again, he had more questions than answers.

There was only one way to find out.

Kieran closed the distance and leaned in to sniff Bradley's neck. He could smell the sweat and anger, but there was no fear. But there was another chemical scent.

"Have you figured it out yet?" Bradley asked.

"What is it?" Kieran snapped back.

"Oh, not all of our research went to waste after you were rescued. I still have a few tricks up my sleeve."

"You won't need sleeves when I rip off your arms," Jackson told him as he slammed Bradley back into the wall.

Bradley grunted in pain, but never stopped smiling.

"You won't kill me," Bradley said. "Neither of you."

He hated this man so much. He wanted to rip out Bradley's throat, but he *was* hesitating. "I wouldn't be too sure about that," Kieran told Bradley.

"But I am," Bradley said. "You want answers. Answers only I can provide."

"That's what the doctor said too. I didn't kill him, by the way, not yet."

Bradley jerked. Kieran also picked up the scent of worry.

"Yep." Kieran leaned close. "I only need one of you."

"Actually," Bradley said, "You only need me. Since the

good doctor doesn't know where Caspar is."

"I'm not falling for that," Kieran told him. "Caspar isn't even in town."

"And he won't be. I have him stashed away."

There was no increase in breathing—his heartbeat remained steady. He didn't appear to be lying.

"We might not be able to kill you, but we can make you hurt," Kieran stated.

Jackson snapped his head to Kieran. "What?"

"I need to verify Caspar's okay," Kieran told him.

Jackson snarled. "But I still get to hurt him?"

"Just don't bite him," Kieran cautioned.

"Why not?" Jackson demanded. "We had a plan!"

"There's something off in his scent," Kieran advised.

"Fine," Jackson muttered, then threw Bradley across the room.

Kieran raced over and picked him back up before tossing him back at Jackson. Jackson laughed as he caught Bradley before lifting him over his head and slamming him down on top of the desk. Jackson's fists were flying so fast Kieran's sight could barely keep up with the punches.

Blood sprayed from Bradley's face, but Kieran didn't stop his friend. Not yet, anyway. He stood back and let Jackson get his revenge. Bradley was a shifter and would be able to heal, although it would take a while. As long as Bradley could talk, that was all Kieran needed.

Jackson roared as he lifted his arm again.

Kieran caught Jackson's wrist. "I think that's enough for now." He nodded at the unconscious man lying on the desk.

"It's not enough. He shouldn't be allowed to live."

Kieran cupped Jackson's face. "We're not killers anymore. Neither one of us. If he doesn't give us the information we need, I can't say we have any use for him, but he will suffer every day he does live."

"I'm pretty sure you broke a guard's neck earlier," Jackson pointed out.

"Yeah." He hadn't forgotten. "But I actually didn't mean

to. We can't murder Bradley just for the sake of killing him."

"I really want to," Jackson said.

"I know, fuck, I know. But we're better than him. Everything we went through and we're not monsters."

"When did you decide this?"

"Earlier, when Dakota stopped me from biting the doctor. I thought I would kill the man instantly the moment I saw him, but I didn't. Shit, I can't explain it."

"It's because as hard as you try to fight it, you really are a good man," Jackson said.

Kieran snorted. "I'm not a saint, so don't make me out to be one."

"Yeah, but, K," Jackson said and dropped to his knees, "We got him. Tell me it's over. I need to hear the words come from you."

Kieran pulled Jackson close and held him. "We got him. It's over." He repeated the words until Jackson was saying them with him.

"I'm okay now," Jackson assured him.

Kieran patted Jackson's back a few times before releasing his friend. He stood up and bent over Bradley's prone body. "Allow me to carry him out." He grabbed Bradley's hair and dragged him off the desk then walked to the door.

Kieran towed the eagle shifter behind him and through the bodies of the guards that were still out. "I can hear others coming," Kieran informed Jackson.

Jackson nodded before he kicked one of the shifter guards in the ribs.

"Really?" Kieran asked with a laugh.

"Just making sure he's still out."

Just as Kieran reached the gap, two Organization agents barreled through. They stopped as they spotted Kieran and Jackson. Kieran vaguely recognized them, but that didn't matter.

"Secure all the guards and get them transported to the office. We'll want to question them as soon as possible," Kieran ordered them.

"Yes, sir," one of the agents replied. "We'll get it done personally."

Kieran nodded and waited until they stepped to the side before dragging Bradley through the opening. He could hear a lot more activity echoing through the caves than before. There was a full-on Organization operation happening. It sounded like their backup had arrived. That meant the kidnapped shifters must have been found.

"We saved them," Kieran whispered. It was a reminder this was about more than what had happened to him and Jackson. If Kieran hadn't been captured and tortured all those years ago, then he wouldn't have known where or how to find the shifters and Alex this time.

Both Bradley and the doctor had a lot to answer for. But Kieran would keep his promise to Jackson too. Bradley wouldn't get the chance to hurt anyone ever again. Once Kieran got the answers he needed, he would end Bradley's life and the doctor's as well. They'd unleashed too much horror onto others to be able to live out the rest of their lives. Even lives in an Organization jail.

When he reached the center room, he saw Dakota helping a wolf shifter and Damon carrying Alex.

"Alex!" Jackson pushed past Kieran and raced to his friend.

Dakota looked over at him then down at Bradley. She smiled. "You got him."

"Yep." Kieran let Bradley drop from his grasp. "And he's going to give me answers."

She nodded. "I know."

The young shifter leaning on her swayed and she tightened her grip. Kieran went to go for her, but Dakota shook her head. "I've got Max. You make sure Bradley gets transported back to the office. Gabe and Dare already have the doctor."

"You sure?" She looked exhausted to him.

"Yeah," she assured him. "I'll meet you back at the office."

He nodded. Dakota smiled at him again before murmuring

to the wolf shifter she was helping. They shuffled forward. Jackson held Alex in his arms and the look of relief was apparent.

Kieran bent down and grabbed Bradley by the back of his neck. He let most of Bradley's body scrape against the cave the entire time he dragged him out. Once he was in the fresh air again, Kieran realized just how bad the scents inside the cave were.

The sun shone down on him bright and hot. They must have been inside for hours, even though it hadn't seemed that long. He lifted his face to the sky and soaked in the warmth. It didn't actually offer him much in the way of heat but, mentally, it helped.

There had been a time when he'd thought he would never see the sun again. At first the doctor had tried to figure out the whole vampires-plus-sun myth, but that had quickly been abandoned. The doctor had been more impressed by the speed at which Kieran healed.

Kieran didn't understand the experiments the doctor had been doing and he didn't want to. The entire idea of mixing shifter and Walker genes was just crazy. A person couldn't be turned into either, had to be born with the gift, so he didn't know what the outcome of the so-called research would even be. Kieran found the thought very disturbing.

"Hey, you okay?"

Kieran looked over to Remy. "Fine, you?"

"Good," Remy answered. "We found Alex and some of the shifters."

"Just some?"

"We recovered the bodies of the rest. We were right. There were more than we originally thought. I don't know if they weren't reported missing or what, but we have a dozen dead."

"Jesus." Kieran felt ill. "They killed that many?"

"Yeah."

He still had a hold on Bradley. Kieran lifted him up to look at the despicable face of a monster. He roared and threw Bradley. He hit the side of an SUV, denting it.

"K!" Remy grabbed his arm.

"Why would they do this?" Kieran asked.

"I don't know but we'll find out. They didn't get away this time."

"No, they didn't." Kieran stomped back to the SUV then grabbed Bradley. He pulled open the back door and tossed Bradley inside. After he slammed the door closed, he looked at his partner. "Are you coming with me?"

"Well, you're not going alone. Someone needs to make sure you don't kill him on the drive."

Kieran only grunted. He yanked open the driver's side door and was relieved to see the keys still in the ignition. He sat as Remy climbed into the passenger seat.

"Start trying to get hold of Caspar," Kieran ordered his partner.

"Caspar? He should be here by now and he's going to be pissed."

"He's not here."

"Well, not here, but I bet he's at the office getting his ass reamed by Sparro."

"No, not in town," Kieran said. "Bradley has him stashed somewhere."

Remy leaned to peer into the back seat. "That guy had our boss kidnapped?"

"Yeah," Kieran replied. "And that's the only reason he's still alive."

Remy unclasped his seatbelt and leaned farther across the seat. He punched Bradley a few times.

"What are you doing?" Kieran asked.

"Making myself feel better," Remy said and hit Bradley again. "Okay." He settled back into his seat and buckled up again.

Kieran backed the vehicle up then slammed his foot on the gas. Remy grunted and slapped his hand onto the ceiling. "Shit, man!"

"Just start making the phone calls. We need to find

Caspar."

"I can't believe this," Remy said, but pulled out his cell phone. "We finally catch these bastards and Caspar goes missing?"

"Yeah," Kieran replied. "They were preparing for us to find them."

"I've been thinking about that."

"About what?" Kieran asked.

"I've been reading the files from the Mount Fauna operation."

"Where'd you get them?"

Remy looked out of the window, avoiding his gaze. Kieran hadn't even gotten to see the Organization file himself, well, not the one they held. Jackson had hacked in and gotten copies, and Kieran had been going through them.

"Rem?"

"Caspar emailed them to me right after he left," Remy said.

"Why?"

"He wanted me to see if I could find anything he might have missed. He suspects Bradley was getting help from someone still inside the Organization."

Kieran took a turn too fast and the SUV fishtailed.

"Damn it, man," Remy complained. "Slow down."

"Caspar thinks someone here is involved, doesn't he?" Kieran asked.

"Yeah."

"That's the real reason we were transferred here," Kieran said, but he was working it out on his own instead of asking his partner. "Caspar wanted us in place in case he found Bradley and Bradley talked. All that bullshit about me being here to find Jackson was just a cover."

"Not all of it. He wanted you to have Jackson at your back. He knew you could trust him and he didn't know who else you would be able to."

"Who does he suspect?"

"I don't think now's the time to get into this."

"Who does he suspect?" Kieran yelled.

"Maybe you should pull over and let me drive," Remy suggested.

"Tell me right now or I'll throw you out of this fucking vehicle while I'm still driving," Kieran threatened. His fangs dropped and the steering wheel cracked under his hands.

"Sparro."

"Fuck!" Kieran hollered as he yanked the wheel to pull the SUV over. He sat there panting.

How bad could this get? The questions were really starting to pile up. Still, as long as he had Bradley in his hands then they had a chance to figure things out.

"Why didn't he tell me?" Kieran asked as he calmed.

"He didn't want you ripping Sparro's throat out before we have proof," Remy said with a laugh.

"Good point," Kieran admitted. "Wait! What about Dare and Gabe? They have the doctor."

"No," Remy said. "I trust them and so does Dakota. I can feel they're not involved."

"Still, we can't let the doctor or Bradley out of our sight. If we don't know who we can trust, then we don't trust anyone."

"Kieran," Remy said. "We need help."

"We only trust those who are already working with us. Bradley wasn't warned this time. It's why we caught him. No one knew."

"Okay," Remy agreed. "Just us."

Chapter Nine

Dakota pulled at the neck of the shirt she'd borrowed. She couldn't wait until she made it down to the locker room to shower and dress in her own clothes. But first she needed to finish going over all the paperwork on the rescued shifters they were housing in the medical wing.

Alex had been taken back to the hotel with Jackson and his men to receive blood and be kept under guard.

So, it was just the shifters that had been admitted for observation. With the paperwork in hand, Dakota paced the corridor. There was no record of a young cougar shifter. They were missing her.

"What are you doing?"

Dakota whirled around. "You startled me," she told Remy.

"Sorry." He held up his hands. "Kieran sent me to find you. He wanted to make sure you'd gotten something to eat."

"Yeah." She waved him off. "I will."

"You might want to clean up, too."

"Sure." Dakota glanced down at the files in her hand again. "Was everyone but Alex transported back here?"

"Yes."

"You're sure?" she pressed.

"What's going on?" he asked.

"I saw a female cougar shifter in the cells. She was the first one I talked to. She was gone when I was helping Max out and she's not here now."

"Let me look." Remy held out his hand. "Why don't you go clean up and I'll see what I can find out? I'll meet you in the cafeteria in thirty."

"Yeah," Dakota agreed. "That'd be good." She passed the folders over then turned to go down to the locker room. A hot shower really did sound good.

"Hey, Dakota," Remy called.

"Yes?"

"Have you seen Sparro?"

She turned back to face him. "No, I checked in with his assistant when I got back, but she said he'd called in and had some meetings out of the office today."

"Thanks," Remy said.

"Sure. I'll see you in a little bit." She continued her way downstairs. It was weird Remy had asked about Sparro, but it was also worrisome Sparro wasn't there. This was the biggest case in years and their director was missing.

Dakota took the stairs instead of the elevator. She thudded down them, thinking about her boss. She needed to talk to Kieran and see if he had any ideas. What if Bradley had somehow gotten hold of Sparro?

As she ran down the stairwell, she pulled out her phone to text Kieran.

Sparro missing? Could Bradley have taken him?

She slipped her phone back in her pocket before hitting the door and slamming it open. The ladies' locker room was the first door on the right and she hurried through, glad it was empty.

"Good," she murmured. The alone time would do her some good and help get her head on straight. She hadn't slept much the night before and it had been a rough day with the shifting.

Dakota undressed and dropped her clothes on the bench in front of her locker.

"We need to talk."

"Shit!" She jumped and whirled around. "Don't scare me like that!"

Kieran grinned. "You should use your senses better."

"In the locker room?" she asked. "In a building full of paranormals?"

"Especially here," he said. "I have something to tell you."

"I was going to shower. I still smell like that place." Dakota did her best to hold in a shudder. It would be a long time before she recovered from all she'd seen.

"Okay." He pulled his shirt over his head. "Let's take a shower."

"We're in the women's locker room. At work."

Kieran unbuttoned his pants and let them drop. She watched as he got completely naked.

"This is a really bad idea," she told him. Even to her own ears her words held no conviction.

He strode forward and lifted her off her feet before carrying her toward the showers. Halfway there he started kissing her and Dakota let go of all her worries. She'd just take a minute to enjoy being with him.

Dakota had her arms and legs wrapped around him as she ravished his mouth. He tasted so good, but most importantly he was alive.

After what she'd seen done to some of the shifters who'd died, she had a better idea of what Kieran had lived through. She'd seen the scars, felt them under her fingertips just as she did now, and heard Kieran and Jackson talk about their experiences, but she hadn't known. Not really.

She ripped her mouth away as he stepped into the tiled shower area. There were six showerheads in the large open area. He walked to the closest one and turned on the spray.

"I want it hot," she told him. They both knew she wasn't talking about the temperature. Kieran would be a lot more successful at making her feel clean than the water.

"You'll get it."

Her back hit the wall as he covered her body with his. Dakota arched so she could rub up against him. He nipped and sucked at her neck while she rolled her hips. It was obvious she wasn't the only one feeling desperate for the connection between them. Kieran was already hard as he pinned her.

"You want me?" he teased as he brushed his fingers up against her clit.

"Yes," she hissed.

He plunged one digit inside and Dakota rocked.

"More," she demanded.

Kieran added a second finger, thrusting them in and out. Dakota let her head drop back as Kieran began to play with her. They ended up in the shower together quite often and she loved it.

"I need you," she told him. "Take me."

Kieran withdrew his fingers and grasped the base of his cock. Dakota watched him, licking her lips, trying to keep from begging.

"Hang on to me," Kieran ordered.

Dakota tightened the grip she had to his shoulders.

He threw his head back and roared as he plunged his shaft into her pussy. Dakota cried out in ecstasy and he began to plunder her.

"Harder," she ordered. "I can take it."

Kieran sped up his thrusts, moving her higher up the wall each time he slammed into her. Dakota's nails bit into his shoulder and she could smell his blood. Her vision grew sharper and for the first time ever during sex, she was afraid of losing control.

"Kieran." She whispered his name.

"It's okay," he reassured her as he stopped. "Let your jaguar come to the surface."

"No." She shook her head. It was bad enough that she'd already let her jaguar rule during the fight, but she couldn't give the power over during sex. She didn't want to hurt her lover. "I can't."

"You won't shift. But now your jaguar knows I accept her, she needs to come to the surface."

He sounded so sure. "What are you talking about? How do you know?"

"Instincts," he told her.

Dakota nodded even as she remained unsure. She always loved to feel the jaguar inside, but this new fear changed so many things for her. She could still feel him pulsing inside her and wanted to just let go of her uncertainty to be with him. "Okay." Dakota could try. Kieran was always telling her that he could keep himself safe. This might end up being the biggest test, though.

Kieran rested his forehead against hers as he slowly withdrew. "Let me see all of you." He thrust back in and Dakota kept looking at him. Keeping that connection, their bond, open.

As Kieran began to drive himself deeper, she felt the electric spark that was always between them sizzle and snap.

She tilted her head back and howled as her jaguar came to the surface. Her vision was sharp, her hearing precise and her scent better. The water fell around them with steam rising to surround them in their own world. There was a wildness within not only her body but also her mind. This was her man, her mate. He needed to claim her with his seed and she would feel complete.

Her teeth lengthened, but she didn't shift. Instead she felt more connected to her animal and to him than ever before in her life. Dakota clung to him. She couldn't hold back the sounds, small mewing noises she was certain she'd never made before.

"Look at me!" he demanded.

She raised her gaze. He was beautiful. Dakota gripped the back of his head while keeping his face close.

Kieran spread her legs wider and she bucked her hips to meet each of his frantic strokes. He filled her deep each time and Dakota couldn't hold back any longer. She roared as she climaxed.

He didn't stop or slow down. Instead, as her body went limp, he tightened his hold and drove on. She was so slick from her release that each thrust remained velvety smooth.

Dakota forced his head back and attacked his neck with her tongue, making sure her sharp teeth stayed covered. She did nip at him when he started to tremble.

"Mine!" he yelled, coming within her.

She cried out as he climaxed. Her feelings were swirling around and she didn't know which to hold on to. The exhaustion edged out all other feelings, though. With his shaky legs, he showed he was just as wiped out.

They collapsed down onto the tiles, but luckily she landed on top of him.

"I think you're trying to kill me," she muttered.

"No." He rolled over before bracing himself on his elbows. "I won't ever let you get hurt."

"I know." She cupped his face. "I was only kidding."

He nodded.

"That was intense, though," she said.

"It was the first time we gave our other halves full range together," Kieran mused.

"How'd you know we could do that?"

"It was just a feeling. Ever since I first went into the caves, my instincts seemed heightened, along with my other senses."

"That's strange. Is it something we need to worry about?"

"We have enough to keep us busy right now." Kieran stood, bringing her with him. "Finish cleaning up. We still need to talk."

"My bag's still in my locker. I need my shampoos and soaps." She really didn't want to move, but they'd only have the locker room to themselves for so long before someone else came in. Maybe Kieran would take pity on her. The sex had been his idea, after all.

"I'll get it."

She grinned. He really was amazing to her. As Kieran walked away, Dakota moved back under the spray and let the water wash away the evidence of their lovemaking.

"Here." Kieran handed her a bottle.

Dakota poured some into the palm of her hand before she

began to wash. Kieran stepped up behind her with a bar of soap.

"If you do that, we'll end up rolling around on the tiles again," she told him.

"It'll save time," he replied.

She had to ignore the feel of his hands on her body and that wasn't easy. Dakota finished cleaning up and twisted the knobs to turn off the water. She grabbed the towel Kieran held out to her.

"What do you want to tell me?" she asked.

Kieran motioned his head to the side. "Come on."

Dakota followed him back into the main part of the locker room. Her bag was on the bench with clothes lying on top. She wiped off the water as she walked.

"Caspar is missing," Kieran stated.

Fuck. Dakota shook her head. "So is Sparro."

"But not for the same reasons."

"What does that mean?"

"We have evidence that suggests Sparro has been helping Bradley," Kieran told her as he dressed.

"No." Dakota grabbed her clothes and pulled them on in jerky movements. "I can't believe you'd even say that. I know you don't trust him but—"

"Caspar told Remy. Emailed him the files from Mount Fauna."

"The same ones Jackson gave you?" Dakota knew more than she'd let on.

"Yes," Kieran said. "It's Sparro."

Dakota yanked her shirt on. "I want to see the proof."

"That's the problem. We have evidence, but not the proof we need yet."

"So what are you going to do?"

"Let's go get you something to eat."

"You didn't answer my question." She grabbed his arm. "What are you going to do?"

"I'm going to get the answers out of Bradley and the doctor."

145

"We have trained agents—"

"No!" he yelled. "No one but us gets to talk to any of them. Dean is handling the shifters in the medical unit and Jackson is coming in to help me with Bradley and the doctor."

"But—"

"I only trust our group. Our friends."

She started to argue but thought about what he'd just said. "Our friends?"

"Jackson, Dean, Gabe, Mitch, Remy, even Damon. Those are who we trust."

He might not have noticed the number of people he trusted had grown, but she did.

"Okay, but there's something I have to do," she said.

He nodded.

"There was a female cougar shifter in one of the cages. She was gone by the time I got Max, but she's not here. She never got checked in."

"You think she might still be there?" he asked.

"I have to find out," Dakota said. "Maybe she shifted and is happily roaming the Red Rocks, but if not, then she needs help."

"You don't go alone."

She nodded.

"And you eat first. You'll probably have to shift again."

"Remy is supposed to meet me in the cafeteria."

"Good." He grabbed her hand and drew her to him. Dakota lifted onto her toes and kissed him as he lowered his head.

They parted as someone came into the locker room.

"Uh…" The female agent paused, looking at Kieran.

"We were just leaving," Dakota said, shoving her bag back into the locker.

Kieran started to snicker and she glared at him, which only made him laugh harder. She had to dart back into the shower and grab her soaps and other shower stuff, then dropped them into her locker and slammed it closed.

"Come on, wise guy." She yanked Kieran behind her.

* * * *

"Three hours," Jackson said as he paced next to the table with a scalpel in his hand.

He was a scary sight, but luckily Kieran wasn't the one tied to the table. "Three hours and fifteen minutes to be exact," Kieran corrected from where he had his feet up on the desk inside the interrogation room.

"Stop! Just stop!" Doctor Scott McCall begged. For all the torture the doctor had put them through, he wasn't doing so well himself. He'd already pissed his pants and hadn't stopped talking at all. They'd barely had to put any pressure on him. Which was a real pity, because as much as Kieran would have loved to be brutal, they hadn't had a need for it. Scott was having no trouble giving up info or remembering anything he'd done.

They'd also gotten intel once the doctor had been taken into custody. He'd been fingerprinted and his DNA swabbed, which had all kinds of details popping up from their system.

The man who had tormented them for years had been once a doctor who'd had his license revoked for experimenting on his patients inside the hospital for mental illness where he'd worked. That little titbit hadn't surprised Kieran at all.

Jackson picked up one of the other tools from the tray and laughed. "What else can we use?"

"I made you better," Scott told them.

It was also easier knowing his name now. The mystery being gone helped Kieran really see the doctor clearly for the first time. He might be a monster, but so were many other men and women in the world. He was just a high-priced murderer. The doctor held no secret power over them and finally Kieran wasn't scared.

"I made you better," Scott repeated.

"Better?" Kieran leapt to his feet and leaned over the

doctor. He was tired of hearing that sentence. The really fucked-up thing was the doctor actually believed his own words. "You tried to kill me."

"You'll see," Scott claimed. "You'll be the most powerful Walker in the world. Your instincts will be sharper and you'll need less blood. I improved you."

Jackson went to cut the doctor, but Kieran caught his wrist. This was new information.

"What are you talking about?"

"I added something extra to your DNA. A concoction that includes some traits from shifters. You're the only Walker it worked on though," Scott said. He turned to Jackson. "I thought it was working with you. You showed such promise."

"Then what happened?" Jackson asked.

"You died," Scott told him. "Or at least I thought you were dead. You had no vitals at all."

"So you dumped my body?"

"What was I supposed to do with you?" Scott asked. The man actually seemed confused by the question.

"What did you put in me?" Kieran demanded. He wasn't sure how to feel about this development. If what the doctor was telling him was true, Kieran was even more fucked-up than he'd known.

"Everything and anything I could," Scott replied.

"Oh, that's helpful," Jackson muttered.

"I don't know what took and what didn't," Scott said. "If I had the chance to run some tests—"

Jackson punched the doctor before he could finish the statement. "You won't be doing anything like that ever again. Your time of torturing people is over."

"I don't think so," Scott replied. "I was making a breakthrough. If it worked on Kieran, the reverse should work on the shifters. We can finally be as strong and fast as you."

Kieran shook his head. "That's what you were doing with the shifters this time, wasn't it? You were trying to add

DNA from Walkers into their system."

"I'm close!" Scott screamed. "I could feel how close I was. If I just had a little more time. I needed more samples from a Walker. We took Alex, but he wasn't handling it as well as the two of you. I told Bradley if I could just get you back…"

This time it was Kieran who stopped the rant. He grabbed the doctor by the throat and squeezed. This guy was fucking unbelievable. "You wanted us back?" he asked. "Well, you got us. Even though I'm sure you're going to find being on this side of things feels a lot different."

"I had plans for you," Scott told him. "And your lover. You could have given me the perfect gift. A child from a Walker and a shifter. Think about the possibilities."

Kieran was so filled with rage he began to squeeze tighter without realizing it. The doctor's eyes bulged and his body jerked where it was tied down.

"I won't stop you killing him, you know," Jackson said easily.

Kieran ripped his hand away and turned around. He was tempted to follow through and just end the miserable bastard, but he had to think of the shifters that needed help now. Scott was still useful. That didn't mean Kieran wouldn't put fear into him.

"Tell me something." Kieran leaned close. "What did you and Bradley do to make your blood smell off?"

"It's just some natural ingredients I have. If you drank enough of it, you'd be sick for a few days," Scott answered.

"It made you both sick?"

"Yes, but it's worth it. We didn't want to take the chance of being bitten and drained."

Kieran shook his head. "All the time you spent torturing and experimenting on us and you still don't know anything about us. It's really sad."

"We know you'll lose control eventually," Scott said.

"Get everything you can out of him," Kieran ordered Jackson. He wiped his hand on his pants, trying to remove the feel of the doctor. Next time he would wear gloves. He didn't want his skin anywhere near Scott.

"And then?" Jackson asked. They both knew they wouldn't kill Scott yet, but Kieran liked to play along.

"Whatever you want," Kieran told him. "If you do kill him, make sure it's as slow and painful as possible."

Jackson grinned, showing off his fangs.

"No!" Scott screamed.

"What are you going to do?" Jackson asked, ignoring the doctor.

"I'm going to check to see if our other guest is awake." The medical team had treated Bradley earlier under his watchful eye and he'd put Dean in charge of him while they waited for him to regain consciousness.

"You need me?" Jackson asked.

"Not yet," Kieran assured him. "Take your time."

"I plan to. It won't hurt the good doctor if his visit is extended."

Kieran nodded. "I'll call you when we're ready." He stepped out of the room to Scott's screams. He didn't feel an ounce of remorse. Especially at the comment about his and Dakota's baby.

They were far from even *discussing* children. Hell, Kieran hadn't even told her he loved her yet. But the doctor mentioning their baby and the plans he would have… Jeez, he actually felt ill at the thought.

He spotted Mitch, Jackson's IT guru, sitting with his back to the wall across from the room he'd exited.

"Waiting on your boss?" Kieran asked.

Mitch shrugged. "I didn't have anywhere else to be and Remy asked me to look into something while he's gone."

Remy was still searching for the proof Sparro was connected to Bradley, but he'd also volunteered to accompany Dakota back out to the Red Rocks. Kieran crouched down. "There's probably a more secure area for you to be doing that kind of investigating."

"Yeah." Mitch nodded. "I'm actually going to be taking it back to the hotel with me, but I wanted to catch you as soon as you were available."

Cautious now, Kieran rocked back on his heels. "Why?"

"Well, when I was talking to Remy and Dakota, she suggested you might take me on a tour of the building." Mitch said.

"I don't think now's the best time—"

"She said you were real good about getting into offices no one else could," Mitch interrupted.

"You want in Sparro's office?"

"Yep." Mitch nodded. "And you need to get me in and out."

Huh, Kieran hadn't thought of that yet. If there was evidence, that would be the logical place to look. "Okay."

Mitch grinned and sort of bounced. "Really? Oh, man, that's so cool."

Kieran laughed. He didn't know how old Mitch was, but Kieran hoped Mitch kept that innocence and enthusiasm for a long time. It wasn't usual for Kieran to get to see that, in either Walkers or shifters. "Let's go then, I've got people to torture."

Mitch jumped up. "I don't know if you're kidding or not."

Wow, the kid was really virtuous. He could see why Jackson wanted to keep him that way. "We'll take the stairs."

"Sure." Mitch shoved his laptop into his backpack.

Kieran glanced around the hall, making sure they were still alone. This part of the basement wasn't used a lot as far as he knew. Since the Organization had changed their policies, saying the agents needed to use non-lethal means, interrogating suspects had also slowed down.

Still, there were times like now when the only way to get answers was to get their hands dirty. That was what the Organization did. The Shifter Coalition played it strictly by the book, so it was up to agents like Kieran to deal with shifters like Bradley.

Kieran hadn't come across the agents from the Coalition yet and he was hoping he didn't.

"I'm ready." Mitch bounced on the balls of his feet.

God, he made Kieran feel old. Kieran nodded to the emergency stairwell. "Just follow my lead. If I tell you to get down, do it."

"I'm used to not being seen. It's how I lasted on the streets for so long," Mitch told him.

Kieran pushed the bar to open the door silently. He led the way up the stairs and through the quiet halls of the upper level where Sparro's office was located. Sparro's assistant had stepped away from her desk, which helped them. Kieran didn't think he'd have a problem getting past her, as she remained terrified of him, but this just made things easier.

"Use your speed to get in when I signal you," Kieran whispered.

Mitch nodded. He placed his hands in his pockets and strolled casually down the hall. The stairwell opened to the opposite end from Sparro's office. Unlike the office on the main level, these didn't have windows. So unless someone actually opened the door and stepped out, they wouldn't see him. The security cameras would pick him up, but he couldn't be worried. It wasn't too uncommon for him to be strolling around where he shouldn't be.

One camera pointed at Sparro's door, but as Kieran passed it, he tilted it up to look at the ceiling. Easy enough to do and when the security people came to fix it, he would hear them in the hallway.

As he walked toward Sparro's office, he pulled a small bag out of his pocket. He selected the tool he needed and in less than ten seconds he had Sparro's door open.

He waved his hand behind him and Mitch raced to him and inside the door. Kieran closed it behind them.

"What are you looking for?" Kieran asked.

"It looks like he took his laptop with him, but let's look for some files," Mitch said.

"Okay." Kieran walked to the row of cabinets against the wall while Mitch began pulling out desk drawers.

The cabinets were locked, but Kieran took care of that easily enough. He saw Mitch messing with the locks of the desk drawers and the young man got them open as well.

"Not bad," Kieran commented.

"Alex's been teaching me," Mitch said. "He's good."

Kieran had no doubt. Kieran didn't actually want to know everything Alex, head of Jackson's security, was responsible for. The files Jackson had passed to him that were obviously hacked from the Organization were bad enough.

Kieran started searching through the cabinet, not even knowing what he was looking for.

* * * *

Dakota glanced over at Remy and raised a brow. "Do you smell that?"

"Cougar shifter, female, and she's scared," he said with a nod.

"I knew something was wrong. I never should have left without making sure she was already being transported back."

"It's not your fault," Remy said. "You had your hands full with Max."

Dakota sighed. She still should have followed through on her instincts. She'd promised the young cougar she was safe then failed her.

"Did you find out who she is?" Remy asked.

"Corey Rebel," Dakota answered. "One of the other shifters knew her. She'd been living in the tunnels for three months. Since she'd left an abusive relationship."

"Damn it." Remy shook his head.

"Yeah. She has to be one of the first taken. Everyone I talked to said she was there already when they'd been taken." Guilt ate at her. "I'm going to shift and see if I have better luck in my jaguar form."

"Good idea."

Dakota stepped behind one of the boulders and quickly undressed. She'd had two cheeseburgers and a large order of fries so she was feeling better, but another shift was going to take the rest of her energy. She crouched and called forward her animal.

Once the transformation was complete, she stretched out her body before hopping up onto the boulder.

"I'll grab your clothes," Remy told her, walking over. He stuffed her belongings into the backpack he carried. "Why don't you see what you can pick up?"

Dakota jumped down and circled the entrance of the cave. She could still smell the cougar she was after, but the freshest scent was leading away. Dakota took off at a sprint.

The sun had heated the rocks around her and she could feel it even through her paws. She was picking up another shifter odor. A powerful one. It seemed familiar, but she couldn't place it.

Remy ran behind her, but she couldn't wait for him. The cougar's fear was pushing her along. Dakota leapt through a small gap and stopped. She could smell blood.

She sniffed the ground. It was the cougar's.

The drops were small, but she could be really hurt. Dakota sniffed one last time before she crawled back through the opening. Remy was almost to her. She pawed at the gap.

"Got it," Remy called. "Go ahead."

She nodded before taking off again. She didn't know how long she'd run but was certain it way past anywhere they'd even gotten to search yet.

She heard a roar and froze. That wasn't good.

Dakota glanced over her shoulder but couldn't see Remy anywhere. He'd be able to follow her, but there was no telling how long it would take him unless he shifted. She could wait for him or go ahead.

The sharp cry of the cougar decided the matter for her.

Growling, she ran to find the lost shifter. The sounds of a fight began to echo around her, so she had to use her nose instead of her hearing. Luckily, she was pretty good at tracking.

She slipped and almost fell into a crevasse but managed to dig her claws into a crack. She tried to get traction with her back feet, but it was no use.

Above her, she heard a bark and saw the wolf just before he grabbed the scruff of her neck and lifted her back up.

Dakota butted her head up against Remy's neck in thanks.

He nudged her forward. She needed to be more careful, still fast, but there was a lot of danger around.

A screech pierced the air and she roared in response. Remy scrambled away and she followed. Ahead, just in front of them. As Remy darted around broken pieces of the rock, Dakota leapt and climbed until she came to a small round space.

The cougar was on the ground, cowering, with a large lion standing over her.

Dakota growled and jumped to land next to the lion. She had no idea how he hadn't heard them coming, but it was obvious she'd surprised him. She managed to avoid a swipe of his claw and danced out of the way.

He turned on her as Remy skidded to her side.

She wasn't sure she'd ever seen a lion shifter as big and powerful as this one. Well, except for her boss. *Oh shit.* She peered closer at the shifter.

It couldn't be Sparro. She'd given Mitch permission to look for a connection because she'd known Sparro was innocent.

The lion's eyes widened and it was in recognition.

He leapt at her and she didn't have time to get away. Dakota went down under his massive weight.

Remy howled and jumped on Sparro's back, distracting him enough for Dakota to slip out from his hold. She swung her claws out to catch his stomach, but Sparro smacked her away from him. At the same time Remy went flying and landed with a hard thud. Dakota snarled as Sparro turned back on her.

She tilted her head as she took in her boss. She could smell his blood, but she knew she hadn't managed to hurt him. That was when she saw the deep cuts around his neck.

It appeared the cougar had gotten a piece out of him. Good for her.

Sparro stepped forward and she automatically backed up.

He growled deeply at her and her fur stood up. She might not have ever gone against a shifter this strong before, but she had to get the cougar to safety.

Dakota opened her mouth, let her sharp teeth show and saliva run down her chin. Jaguars were known for their powerful jaws and she was reminding him of that.

Sparro rose and began to stalk toward her. Dakota stayed where she was until she could feel his breath against her face. She snarled and attacked.

She used teeth and claws, all her energy and power, until she was on top of him, tearing out patches of his fur. She let her anger and rage consume her. All those shifters in the cages, abused and hurt. Sparro had been a part of that. He'd helped Bradley. Bradley, the man who had almost killed Kieran!

Blood coated her muzzle, but she still continued to slash at Sparro's neck.

"Stop!"

She heard the words, but they didn't matter. The only important thing was making sure Sparro, Bradley and the others never got the chance to hurt anyone ever again.

"Stop!"

She was jerked off Sparro and tossed against the edge of a boulder. Dakota rolled, panting and shaking.

"You can't kill him." Remy stood naked above Sparro, blocking her from ending him.

She snarled and tried to snap, but her stomach burned. Dakota peered down and saw her own blood coating the ground.

"Shit!" Remy rushed over to her. "You're hurt."

She tried to shake her head, but her vision blurred.

"Fuck, Kieran is going to kill me for letting you get hurt,"

Remy complained.

Dakota whined, but when she tried to rise, her shaky legs gave out on her and she fell back down.

"I'm going to get my bag," Remy said, crouching over her. "I've got to call for backup."

She nodded.

"Sparro's out," he said. "So is the cougar. Just stay here."

He took off and Dakota looked around the small clearing. There was blood staining the ground. She needed to check on the cougar. Her stomach was still stinging, so Dakota started to crawl toward the cougar. Corey, she needed to remember the young woman's name. Corey had fought well. She'd stood up to the powerful lion and Dakota was going to make sure she was okay.

She wouldn't fail her again.

It was hard not to rip out Sparro's throat as she crept past him, but now the adrenaline had ebbed, she was feeling the pain.

After what seemed like forever, Dakota finally dropped down beside the cougar shifter. Corey blinked open her eyes and watched her as Dakota took in the cougar's injuries.

Nothing looked life-threatening and Dakota was beyond relieved. Maybe that was a little less guilt she would carry around, because she knew Corey getting injured was all her fault.

There was no way Dakota could shift in her current condition so she laid her neck against Corey's to offer comfort.

Corey rumbled and nuzzled her back.

Dakota closed her eyes, hoping Remy hurried.

Chapter Ten

Kieran had known Bradley would be tough to get to talk but he was running out of ideas. They'd hung Bradley by his wrists and Jackson and Kieran had taken turns on him, but Bradley still hadn't told them where Caspar was.

No one in the Organization had seen or spoken to Caspar or anyone on his team since he'd left for the airport to come to Vegas. Kieran was past getting really worried.

"Where is Caspar?" Kieran asked Bradley before punching him in the ribs.

At first all Bradley had done was laugh, but his responses had evolved into grunts and curses. He would be broken eventually, Kieran had no doubt, but didn't want to wait.

He howled in pain this time. Kieran was sure they'd broken every rib already but still Bradley didn't tell them what Kieran needed to know.

"Where?" Kieran demanded.

"I don't know!" Bradley screamed.

Kieran let his fangs drop and bit down on Bradley's side. He ravaged the wound, not really wanting to taste the sick fucker's blood but knowing he would weaken Bradley further. The doctor had told Jackson as long as they didn't swallow any blood, they wouldn't get sick. It had been worth the risk to see if the doctor had been lying or not. So far, Kieran wasn't feeling any side effects. Bradley kicked his legs, but Jackson caught them and held him still.

"You better talk," Jackson told him. "We'll drink you dry if we have to."

"I swear I don't know," Bradley claimed. "My guys lost him at the airport. The man I had on Caspar's team hasn't reported in."

Kieran didn't believe Bradley, although all the signs showed he wasn't lying. No one could find any sign of Caspar. Kieran poked his fingers into Bradley's side where he'd bitten. "Why don't we talk about Marcello Sparro?"

Bradley jerked, but Kieran didn't think it was from the pain. He caught the quick burst of surprise in Bradley's scent.

"Didn't think we knew about him, did you?" Kieran asked.

"I haven't spoken to Sparro in—"

Jackson leaned forward and dug his fangs into Bradley's shoulder.

"Don't lie," Kieran advised.

"I can't..." Bradley gasped.

"He's going to pass out again," Jackson observed. "For all his talk back in the cave, he sure does cry like a little baby."

"He's a bitch," Kieran stated. "I knew that the first time I laid eyes on him."

"I can't take it," Bradley shrieked.

"You should have thought about that before you decided to torture people for a living," Jackson advised him as he scraped a knife down Bradley's side. "I'm going to make your skin just as pretty as you made ours. Give you some marks that will never fade."

"I'm telling you the truth!" Bradley screamed. "I don't know where he is."

Kieran held back his frustration. This was getting them nowhere. He'd thought once he had his hands on Bradley and the doctor, he would somehow be fixed. Instead he was finding out it didn't matter what he was told. He'd suffered years of abuse and torture for no other reason except Bradley and the doctor were absolutely crazy.

He was disappointed in more than just them. He shouldn't have thought revenge would solve all his issues. He knew better than that, really, but some part of him had just expected to feel better.

With a look of disgust toward Bradley, he strolled across the room and leaned back against the wall. Jackson followed him over.

"We've gotten more information out of him and the doctor than I thought even possible. For two guys who are supposed to be masterminds, they were really easy to break," Jackson said.

"They don't like the pain, although neither had any issues with causing it."

"He's admitted to everything else," Jackson pointed out. "Or we knew he was lying. What if he doesn't have Caspar?"

"Then where the hell is he?" Kieran wouldn't stop until he'd seen his boss. If it wasn't for Caspar, then Kieran wouldn't have been able to survive at all. The thought of Caspar being treated like he had made Kieran want to go on a rampage and kill everyone he suspected of being involved.

"I don't know," Jackson said. "But unless you really do want to kill Bradley, we need to let him rest."

Kieran turned his wrist and was shocked to see they'd been questioning Bradley for over five hours. They were well into the evening. "I want to call Dakota anyway. I can't believe she hasn't checked in with me."

"I'm going to take a break before I go visit the doctor again. Dean needs some more information about what he did to the shifters."

"Sounds good." Kieran pushed himself off the wall. "I'll have someone secure Bradley for the night. We'll start fresh with him after we get some sleep."

"Okay," Jackson agreed.

Kieran pulled open the door and was surprised to see Remy, Gabe, Dare and Mitch waiting in the hall.

"What happened? Is it the doctor? If he got away, I'll kill you all." Kieran stomped forward. "We still need answers from him."

"Jackson's guys are standing guard. The doc is still right

where you left him," Remy said.

Kieran rolled her shoulders as he prepared for bad news still. "But?"

"We found Sparro," Remy told him.

"Is he alive?"

"Yes, he's in the medical wing being looked at."

"And the cougar?"

"She's fine, with the others being looked after."

"Then what—" *Fuck, no, no, no!* "Where is Dakota?" he asked as calmly as possible. He grabbed Remy by his shirt and lifted his partner off the ground. "What happened to her?"

Remy wrapped his hands around Kieran's. "She's fine."

There was no scent of deceit in Remy's words. "Where is she?" Kieran's demanded.

"In one of the medical rooms."

Kieran didn't even give Remy a chance to say more. He bolted for the closest stairwell that would take him upstairs. He should have gone with her instead of sending his partner. If he hadn't been so worried about breaking the doctor or Bradley, then Dakota wouldn't be hurt.

There was no reason she should be in medical. She was a shifter and it took a lot for her to be seriously injured. But if Sparro was also being checked out, then that meant Dakota had tried to take him on.

Holy shit! As well trained as Dakota was, Sparro was one of the strongest shifters that Kieran had ever seen. Even Kieran had struggled with the lion shifter the first time they'd met.

He practically flew up the steps until he reached the second level. Kieran threw open the door, startling several of the agents around him. They quickly scrambled out of his way as he raced past them.

There was no one in the halls of the medical wing, but he didn't need to talk to anyone. He followed the scent of Dakota, her blood, to the fourth door. Just as he was about to tear through the door, it opened and Dean stepped out.

They both grunted as they collided, but while Kieran kept on his feet, Dean bounced back into the room.

"What the hell?" Dakota asked.

She was leaning against the bed, holding on to it and staring at Dean. When she looked up at him, Kieran lost his breath.

"You're okay," he stated.

"Yeah." She frowned at him. "Didn't Remy tell you that?"

Well, his partner had tried, but Kieran had freaked out. He stepped into the room and let the door shut behind him. "You're really okay?" he asked this time.

"I'm okay too," Dean muttered as he picked himself up off the ground.

"Sorry." Kieran reached down and helped the human onto his feet.

"Sure." Dean patted his shoulder. "I'll give you a minute to talk. I'm going to check on Sparro."

As soon as they were alone, Kieran grasped Dakota's upper arms and looked her over. "What happened?"

She sighed before lifting up her shirt. There were several gouges on her stomach.

"I'll kill him," Kieran stated firmly.

"I almost did. I'm fine and I found the cougar shifter before Sparro could kill her."

"So he's involved? You have proof?" he asked.

"Well, since I have these" — she waved at her body — "I'm going to say he knows he's screwed."

"I should have been there," Kieran told her as he yanked her into a hug.

She hissed but wrapped her arms around his back. "This isn't your fault. So don't start blaming yourself. I lost control, almost killed him and didn't notice I was injured until Remy stopped me."

Kieran pulled back a little so he could peer down at her. Her words surprised him, since Dakota never lost control.

"All I could think about was how he was involved in what you went through, what the others are trying to recover from, and I let my jaguar take over." She shook her head. "I just lost it, Kieran."

"I don't care." His only concern was that she was in front of him and while she'd been injured, she was in his arms, where she belonged.

"I do," she whispered. "I can't help the others if I can't rein my jaguar in."

"Control? That can be taught. Trust me. What they really need is someone who believes in them, will fight for them and make sure nothing like this ever happens to anyone else."

"Is that what helped you?"

"Yeah," Kieran answered. "Caspar saved me. I was so grateful to be out of that hellhole I would have done anything for him. And all he wanted was for me to heal."

"We'll help them heal too," she said.

Kieran nodded then kissed her forehead. Her sweet scent surrounded him and he simply breathed her in. Even with the sweat and blood, the underlying aroma was pure Dakota.

Maybe he wasn't as broken as he'd thought.

The need for revenge, the last threads, slowly vaporized.

Dakota loved him the way he was. All his flaws and issues and still she chose to be with him. He didn't need to change. The acceptance in her touch was enough.

For the first time since he'd been grabbed on that dark night when he'd been eighteen, he let go of all his worry and fear. He could lean on her and she would catch him.

He also had Remy and Jackson, their friends—the family he'd made in less than a month.

"I love you," he whispered in her ear.

Dakota laughed before tilting her head back. "I know. I love you too."

He kissed her then, deep and wet. He put all his feelings, the relief, the need to comfort, to protect, into his lips as they met hers. Kieran grew lightheaded but didn't pull back until he had no choice but to breathe.

They jumped at the knock on the door. Neither of them had been paying attention to their surroundings.

"You're not naked, are you?" Dean called through the door.

Dakota huffed as she dropped her head on his chest. "And I was starting to miss him as a partner."

Kieran laughed. "We're dressed," he hollered back at Dean.

The door opened and Dean stuck his head through the gap. "Sorry to interrupt, but Jackson needs you back downstairs."

Kieran stiffened. "What happened?" Jeez, would this night ever end? They had to stop going in fucking circles and he was tired.

"Not sure," Dean answered. "He said it wasn't an emergency but as soon as you got a chance you should go back down."

What could have happened in the few minutes he'd been gone? Kieran wasn't sure he wanted to know.

"Let's go see what Jackson needs." Dakota pulled on his hand.

"You should rest. Lie back down," Kieran said. Her wounds weren't bleeding, but he didn't want to take any chances with her.

She laughed in response. "I'm not lying around while everyone else figures out what's going on. Let's see what Jackson needs and go home."

Dean sighed. "You really should take it easy."

"Fine," Dakota snapped. "I'll sit in the corner and watch Kieran torture someone. That should be a fun date."

Kieran barked out a laugh. Fuck, he was rubbing off on Dakota and he loved it.

"Do you want me to bring you some popcorn?" Dean snarked.

"I wouldn't mind a pizza," she replied with a wink.

Kieran's stomach growled.

"Jesus!" Dean threw his hands up in the air. "I'll feed you

both. It's like I'm the only responsible person in this place." He stomped off down the hall.

Dakota slapped her hand over his mouth and Kieran raised an eyebrow.

"I don't even want to know how you would respond to that," she said.

Kieran licked her hand.

"Damn it!" She pulled her palm away and rubbed it on her sweatpants. "I should have seen that coming."

"You really should have," he agreed. Kieran wrapped his arm around her waist as he led her down the hall. "Let's take the elevator."

"You never take the elevator," she argued.

"I can kiss you in it," Kieran whispered in her ear.

"Security cameras," she reminded him.

He snorted. "You put our boss in the medical ward. Who's going to say anything?"

"Oh." Dakota's amusement fled. "I don't know who to call. Shouldn't we let someone know?"

Well damn. Kieran hadn't thought about that. He punched the button to call up the elevator and it opened right away.

"Maybe Dean will know," she said pulling out her phone from one of her pockets. "I'll text him."

Kieran waited until she was done and had put her cell back before he gently pushed her inside the elevator and against the wall to kiss her. She wrapped her arms around his neck as he plunged his tongue into her mouth.

The sweats were tight around her ass he used the opportunity to run his palms down her back to cup her butt. She moaned and he swallowed the sound while leaning harder into her.

"That's hot."

Kieran ripped his mouth away and glanced over his shoulder to see Remy and Mitch watching them from the open elevator doors. It had been the young Walker who'd spoken.

"Don't make me gouge your eyes out," he threatened.

Mitch grinned back.

"Come on," he said to Dakota, ushering her out in front of him. The hallway was empty except for Mitch and Remy, so Kieran turned back to his partner. "What's going on?"

Remy nodded toward the room Bradley was being held in. "Go ahead."

He strained to hear something, but it was quiet. "What?"

"God, you are so untrusting. Open the door and go inside. There's a surprise waiting for you," Remy said.

"Bradley's guts are probably strung across the room," Kieran muttered but walked to the closed door. He didn't waste time and opened it enough so he could slip through. If Jackson had torn Bradley apart, Kieran didn't want Dakota to see it.

Jackson was sitting in a chair smiling and another man was standing in front of Bradley. He turned and Kieran gasped. "*Caspar?*"

"Hey, K," Caspar greeted. "I thought I told you to wait for me."

"Uh…" Kieran was at a loss for words.

"I figured you'd ignore my order, but I thought at least Remy was smart enough—"

"Where the fuck have you been?" Kieran shouted. He was shaking and he didn't know how else to show his relief. Caspar was fucking standing in front of him, not stuck in a cage being tortured.

"It's a long story," Caspar told him. "We'll catch up later."

"I'll take the CliffsNotes version," Kieran demanded. He folded his arms across his chest and glared.

Caspar grinned in response. "Really?"

Okay, he couldn't intimidate his boss. "What happened?" he asked softly.

Caspar sighed but walked to him. "I picked up the tail Bradley had on me at the airport. I lost him, but it also meant I missed my flight. I went to rent a car and someone on my own team tried to take me out. I was surprised and even with my guard up I wasn't prepared for the ambush from my own man. He had help and the other guy managed to knock me out and stuff me in the trunk of my own rental car." Caspar rubbed the back of his head. "That still pisses me off."

Oh, Kieran would bet it did. "What happened to the guy on your team?"

"He won't be betraying anyone else ever again."

Kieran nodded his approval.

"The guy who did manage to knock me out wasn't as professional or well versed in kidnapping as Bradley's other guys. When the punk stopped for gas, I used the trunk release to get out and put him in the trunk. We were already headed in this direction. The kid's in lock-up."

"You couldn't call?" Kieran shouted.

"I lost my cell phone at the airport and I didn't want to go through the office here. I figured I would catch up with you when I got to town. Which is what I'm doing," Caspar explained.

Kieran huffed. "You could have fucking called." Then because he sounded like a bratty child he added, "Remy was worried about you."

"I know." Caspar patted his shoulder before pulling Kieran into a hug. "But I'm here now."

"It's a good thing too, because I'm about worn-out for the night," Jackson said.

Kieran let go of Caspar. "Me too."

"Is Dakota all right?" Jackson asked as he strolled forward.

"Yeah, some pretty bad cuts on her stomach, but she'll be okay," Kieran replied.

"I'm still a little surprised she managed to take down Sparro," Caspar said.

"You know about that?" Kieran asked.

"Remy filled me in when I got here. I already called his boss and I've been put in place until this mess can be cleaned up. We'll be getting some agents and directors from other offices flooding in soon."

Kieran turned his lip up in disgust.

"I also called the Coalition, who will be back in the morning to take care of the injured shifters."

"Why?" Kieran asked. "They're already here."

"Because we have a clusterfuck to clean up and we don't need to worry about the medical part. The Coalition have trained staff that can handle this. They agreed to take care of that part of the investigation and work with our lab while we handle getting everything we can from Bradley, Sparro and the others," Caspar informed him.

"There's a cougar shifter that Dakota—"

"I've been made aware of that situation. The young woman—Corey, I believe her name is—will be staying here since she's the only one we can connect with Sparro so far," Caspar said. "We're letting her rest right now, but after she's been questioned, we'll figure out what to do with her."

Kieran relaxed. With Caspar back and taking control, he could finally breathe, for real. He wasn't the one who had to make all the decisions. He wasn't a leader, or at least he didn't want to be. His place was out on the streets, tracking down criminals.

Caspar nodded as if he knew what Kieran was thinking. "I'm trained for this."

"Thank God," Kieran murmured.

"Right now I want the two of you and the rest of your team to go home. Eat, sleep, have sex, I don't care what you do but I don't want to see you before eight tomorrow morning," Caspar ordered.

"About that." Jackson motioned to Bradley. "I don't work for you, but—"

"You'll be brought in as a consultant, as well as your IT kid," Caspar finished for him. "It's the least I can do."

"Can you even authorize that?" Kieran asked. "They're civilians."

The look Caspar sent him spoke volumes. Not only was Caspar authorized, but he'd be doing whatever he damned well felt like. It seemed his boss was back in more ways than just physical. Shit, Kieran was so relieved. He actually felt as though a weight had been lifted off his shoulders.

"I'll accept, but I'll have to ask Mitch if he's okay with it," Jackson said.

"That's fine," Caspar agreed. "But you can tell me tomorrow. You both look like something the dog chewed up and spit out."

Kieran grinned and opened the door. "I won't tell Remy you're telling jokes about him."

"I can hear you both, you assholes," Remy called.

"Get out of here," Caspar ordered.

Kieran strolled to Dakota. "Let's go home. We'll order room service before we get in the shower."

She leaned against him. "Sounds good to me."

Chapter Eleven

Three days later

"Dakota?" Kieran walked into their suite and hollered for his lover. He was beyond exhausted and just wanted a hot shower with a hotter woman. He heard claws clatter against the bathroom floor and grinned. She'd been shifting every day to help speed up her healing, but he'd missed it. Looked like he'd timed it perfectly this time.

He could hear the shower running as he strolled toward the open bedroom door. Kieran pulled off his jacket and tossed it over a chair as he passed. The bathroom door stood open, but steam billowed out. He peered around the jamb and saw Dakota half in the shower, half out, looking like she was getting ready to shift back to human.

"No," he told her quickly. "Don't change back yet."

She huffed at him.

"So is this what you do while I'm at work all night? Play in the water?" he teased.

She swiped at him with her massive paw, but he caught it. It was still strange to him to see her in her jaguar form, but he found he actually enjoyed it. He knew she was still uncertain, evidenced by the fact that she hadn't been shifting in front of him, but he was going to get her to see he accepted every part of her.

Dakota's injuries from the fight with Sparro were almost healed, but she was still struggling with the fact she'd lost control and almost killed him. Kieran didn't know how to help her deal with it, other than to hold her when she woke from nightmares.

Their roles had reversed. Kieran was accepting he was a flawed individual and it was up to him to change his future. Without even realizing it, he'd begun to take back control of his life. He'd formed bonds with his partner and boss, he'd fallen in love with Dakota, reconnected with Jackson and was making new friends like Alex and Dean. He also had a soft spot for Mitch, the young Walker. All of these people had become family to him. His choice of who he wanted to be with.

Dakota had done the reverse. She'd distanced herself from the same people who Kieran had grown to care about.

The only one she wanted to be around was Kieran, but only in her human form. Everyone had called or stopped by, but she'd refused to see them. She went into the office to check on Corey but wouldn't talk to anyone else. It was as if she was turning into a different person.

He had to find a way to bring her back to him, to all of them, while making her forgive herself.

"Well, if you want to play, let's play," Kieran told her.

She shook her head before backing away. Of course, that had her going to the spray of water.

"Why not?" he asked. "You told me last night you wanted to play in the shower in your jaguar form. I said it could be fun."

Dakota whined at him when took a step.

"You're afraid." He stopped. He hadn't noticed the scent before, since she was wet and that odor took up most of his senses.

She whined again.

"You won't hurt me. I know you're afraid of losing control again but it won't happen."

When she opened her powerful jaw, showing off her sharp teeth, he chuckled. "You don't scare me either."

This time she shook her entire body, which made the water on her coat fly everywhere, even onto him. Since he was already wet, he followed her into the stall and let them both get soaked. He was forcing the issue, but something had to change and this was the only thing he could think of.

Dakota had backed herself into the corner, so Kieran sat on the floor across from her. She tilted her head.

"I can stay here all night," he told her. "With the water this warm, it will actually be better than usual."

Dakota lifted her paw and slapped it down into a puddle that had formed. The splash drenched him.

"Oh yeah?" he taunted and stood to palm one of the showerheads. Dakota cocked her head and he let go. The shift in direction of the spout had the water flowing right at her face.

With a happy cry, she bounced.

"You like that, do you?" He stretched, grabbed at one of the higher streams and positioned it toward her face.

It was incredible. Dakota transformed from a scared shifter to a playful cat. She hopped and jumped, trying to get to the water. Kieran laughed along with her. A spark of inspiration hit and he grabbed the shower gel and squeezed it in front of one of the streams. The small space filled with bubbles. Dakota roared and chased one until it popped. Another floated in front of her and she swung at it.

Kieran would never have believed she could be this lighthearted after how she'd been feeling. She must have really needed this. Dakota was slipping and sliding but still tried to catch all the suds. She hit the edge of the stall, cracking the trim, but didn't seem to notice. He might have to pay for the repairs, but it would be worth it.

He followed her out, grabbing a towel as he walked behind her. She was still leaping around the bedroom, then stopped suddenly. He made a move to go to her, but she dropped down onto the carpet and rolled onto her back.

She was adorable wiggling around and scratching an itch she couldn't quite reach. Kieran laughed before he knelt beside her.

"Let me help," he told her.

Dakota froze with her bright eyes staring back at him.

"You won't hurt me," he promised. Slowly he placed

his hand on her stomach and rubbed. She gave something between a moan and a gasp so he stroked her harder. "See, I told you."

She allowed him to massage her entire belly and legs before she flipped over. Kieran started at her shoulder blades and scratched. Dakota made all kinds of noise until finally she just collapsed.

"Are you ready to shift back?" he asked quietly.

She blinked then nodded. He gave her just enough space to transform. He felt the movement in the air before she was sprawled out on the carpet.

"There you are," he whispered.

"I could have killed you," she said.

"As I told you before, I won't have a problem stopping you. You can't hurt me," Kieran argued.

She sighed. "You shouldn't have taken the chance. I would have never forgiven myself if I'd hurt you."

"You are already living with guilt as it is."

She started to get up but he grabbed her shoulder and forced her back down.

"I don't want to talk about it."

"Tough," he told her. "It's been three days."

"And I'm just supposed to forget I almost killed my boss? That I lost control of my jaguar!"

"What bothers you more? That it was Sparro? Or your supposed loss of control?" Kieran asked.

"Don't mock me," she snarled. "Don't you fucking dare!"

"I'm not," he answered truthfully. "I'm just trying to make you see this was no different than any other time you had to take out a shifter."

There was silence for several moments. "But I haven't."

He frowned. "Haven't what?"

"Killed a shifter or anyone," she confessed. She stared at the wall behind him.

"Really?" Kieran didn't know how any Organization agent could have gone so long without having to take someone out.

"It's not part of my job. I investigate," she explained.

Kieran nodded. "Okay, good. Well, you still haven't."

"You don't understand."

"No," he agreed. "Because I have killed. It was always in the line of duty or to save a life. The same as it would have been for you."

Tears pooled in her eyes.

"You were injured and didn't know the condition of Corey or Remy. You were scared and that's okay. I have no doubt you would have made the right choice. No doubt."

"You believe in me?" she asked. "That much?"

"Always," he replied. He wiped away one of the tears that fell. "Always."

"I am so scared of losing control."

"I will be here to help you," he promised. "If you want to practice control or learn to fight better in human form. Whatever it is you need. Let me help you."

"We'll do it together," she said.

"We already are."

"Okay." She rolled on top of him, her naked body covering his wet one. "Your clothes are soaked."

"Someone was playing in the shower when I got home," he responded with a smirk.

"I wasn't expecting you back so soon."

He snorted. "That was obvious."

"You have to be cold."

Now she'd said the words, he could feel the chill seeping into him. "Yeah."

"I should warm you up." Dakota undressed him, then they crawled into the bed. She lay over him, stroking his cock.

"I was thinking we should get a more permanent place," Kieran began.

"You want to discuss this now?" she asked.

Kieran almost told her no when she trailed kisses down his chest. "It's been on my mind."

"We don't have to move," she said. "I love it here." Dakota

174

crouched over him, still rubbing his shaft.

"It's a hotel suite. We rent it, even if I'm not paying for it, and we should have something that's ours."

"Then talk to Jackson about one of the residences for sale here."

"What?" he asked, growing distracted.

"Jackson owns his own rooms. So do some of his men. He was going to talk to you about it when he was sure you would stay in town."

"I'm staying," he swore. "I won't ever leave you."

"Especially now Caspar has been appointed acting director," Dakota teased.

"Well, that doesn't hurt, but even if Caspar hadn't decided to stay, I wouldn't have left you."

She laughed. "Like you have any control. I would hunt you down."

"How about you forget about hunting and suck me instead," he suggested.

Her laughter rang out. "I might do that," she said. "But first I'm going to bathe you in my scent. You might not have a smell, but I'll have fun trying."

Kieran spread his arms out wide. "I'm under your control."

Pack Alpha

Excerpt

Chapter One

Cool wind whipped the fur around her face as she leapt over a log to land easily on her paws. She could smell the water from the creek ahead as well as the damp soil and other critters running around.

As she slowed down, her heart continued to beat frantically. Movement to her left drew her attention. A powerful male wolf stepped into view. She almost stumbled from the power that radiated from the shifter.

Instinct had her dropping down to her belly as the wolf strode toward her. She rested her chin on her front paws to show the appropriate amount of submission. She didn't want to challenge this male—no, indeed, her body was reacting to his dominance by tightening in arousal. He lowered his head while he was still several yards away and she got the distinct impression that he was scenting her.

She rolled over onto her back and tucked her paws close to her chest, showing him that she was completely open to him. When he finally reached her he used his snout to push her paws aside and nuzzled the soft vulnerable skin of her belly. She whimpered in both obedience and need. He rewarded her with a lick across her muzzle before he gave her side a strong push, causing her to roll.

He braced himself over her back and she knew what would come next. She lifted her rear end up into the air to accept him.

Marissa Boyd gasped as she was startled awake. She panted, turned on from her erotic dream, and her entire body flushed and hot. Fuck, that had been wild.

Next to her, the man she'd picked up at the bar the night before was snoring softly. Damn, she'd forgotten about him.

She climbed out of her king-sized bed quietly, hoping not to disturb her sleeping partner. Hell, she wished they had gone back to his place instead of hers, then she could have slipped away without having to face him again. Instead, she was going to have to do the whole 'Good morning, had a great time, don't call me, I'll call you' thing. And with that dream still affecting her it would be hard to act normal.

The bedroom door was open so she strolled out naked and straight to the living area. At least there she had a basket of clean clothes that she hadn't put away yet. She picked up a pair of panties then slipped them on before grabbing a T-shirt and pulling it over her head. Once she was covered she walked over to the large windows and yanked open the curtains. She had a beautiful view of the Pacific Ocean and she enjoyed seeing it when the sun was just rising over the water.

Even though she'd lived there for a few years now she wasn't used to seeing all the openness. The Pack that she'd grown up in had been located in the middle of the woods. She'd given up the freedom of nature to surround herself with water and city people.

Marissa pressed her hand against the cool pane of glass and closed her eyes. Why did she have to dream about things that she would never have? It was impossible for her to ever have her fantasies become reality. She was alone and she should be used to that, but Marissa craved the intimate touch of someone who would accept her. Even if she was broken. She'd been on her own for so long now that she figured the feelings of loneliness would have disappeared. Instead the feeling was stronger than ever.

But she was a grown woman and didn't have time to let her despair rise. She pushed off the window and turned to go into the kitchen. It was only a dream and she would forget about that and the male wolf that didn't exist. At least not for her. The coffee pot was ready to go so all she had to do was press the power button. After she got some caffeine inside her she could get rid of her guest.

If I could only remember his name.

Damn, she hated when the full moon was close. It was the only time she didn't have complete control over her shifter side. Marissa might be defective but she did get horny around this time of month like so many of the other shifters. She didn't know if it was a wolf thing or what. It wasn't like she could ask anyone either. Her family was gone except for her sister, Elizabeth. And Marissa would not be asking her sister about her sex life. Elizabeth was much more conservative than she was.

The beep from the machine let her know that her coffee was ready. She strolled back over to the counter then reached up and pulled down a mug. Marissa poured some of the dark brew into the cup before adding some sugar. She stirred it slowly as she breathed in the fragrant aroma. If there was anything that she spent too much money on it was her organic and expensive coffee — a habit she had picked up when she'd first moved into the small coastal town. She lifted the mug to her lips and blew on the liquid inside, then took a sip.

"Ah," she murmured in happiness.

"That smells great. Can I get a cup?"

She jerked slightly, not having heard her companion wake and walk around her condo. She turned and smiled at him. Damn, he was built. He had long black hair with beautiful blue eyes. His chest, arms and back were muscular and he had a hard six-pack. Yeah, she'd picked damn well the night before. She licked her lips as he stood there in just a pair of jeans, still unbuttoned, and looking sexy as hell.

Chad, she could remember his name now. They'd met at the local bar that she liked to visit because it had rough, biker-type patrons. For a human he sure had given her one hell of a ride.

"Sure." She waved him forward. "Come on in."

He grinned, showing perfectly straight white teeth.

Hmm, maybe she could take him back to bed for an encore. If the dream could help with anything maybe it would get her into the right mood. Chad was nothing like the wolf in her dream. Of course, he was human, but he also couldn't force her to submit the way that only a strong shifter male could. Still, it would be a waste to send him away while she was tingling with need. She'd make his drink and let things grow from there.

"How do you take your coffee?" she asked.

"Black is fine," he replied against her ear as he stepped up behind her.

She shivered slightly from the huskiness of his voice. Marissa grabbed another mug then filled it up before she turned to face him.

The look in his eye was telling her he wouldn't mind another round either. She handed him the cup, making sure to let her fingers brush his. He accepted it with his right hand but wrapped his left around her back. He pulled her close as he dipped his head.

"I really enjoyed last night," he said.

"Me too," she agreed. Marissa ran her hand over his naked chest. "You sure know how to show a girl a good time."

He chuckled. "It's easy when I'm with the right partner."

Marissa flushed. Yeah, she had been up for anything with the full moon just a day away. Chad nuzzled her neck then gave her a quick nip. The move was so unexpected that she jumped. It was almost wolf-like. She knew he was human but that small sting was perfect. A repeat was very much needed indeed. He set his mug down on the countertop with a loud clunk before he gripped her hips, lifting her up.

As she landed on the marble top he stepped between her legs. Marissa was glad she hadn't gotten completely dressed. She ran her hand over the muscles on his chest then bent forward and licked one of his nipples. He groaned while threading his fingers through her hair. Marissa scooted closer to the edge so she could get a better angle. While tracing her tongue from one pec to the other, she trailed her hands down his stomach toward the waistband of his jeans.

"Yeah," he murmured and rocked his hips as she slid her hands into the denim.

He was fully erect and she wanted to get a taste.

A loud banging on her front door stopped her from dropping into position.

Chad groaned but helped her slide off the counter. She offered him a smile then patted his chest before she headed toward the door. A glance at the clock in the living room showed her that it was just after nine in the morning. Marissa had no idea who would be at her place so early on a Saturday morning. What if she wanted to sleep in? That was just rude.

When she reached the front door she looked out of the peephole to see who was there. A young man in a brown shirt and shorts stood shuffling his feet while holding an envelope. She wasn't expecting a delivery but unlocked and opened the door anyway. Maybe the kid had the wrong address.

"Yes?" she asked.

"Marissa Boyd?" the young man asked.

"Yes."

"I have an overnight letter for you," he said.

"From who?" Why would anyone send a letter through a service that would cost so much?

The kid glanced down at the notepad in his other hand. "It's from an Elizabeth Boyd in Texas."

Her sister. Now Marissa was really curious. "Okay," she said, reaching out for the envelope.

"I need you to sign this, please." He offered her the clipboard with a pen attached by a string.

Marissa smiled as she signed her name quickly then handed it back. The young man passed her the envelope. It was pretty light so it didn't seem to have anything big in it. "Thanks," she murmured but wasn't really paying the delivery kid any more attention. She closed the door and shook the package.

"Everything okay?" Chad asked from the kitchen doorway.

"Hmm," she responded distractedly, starting to tear open the package. She shook out a smaller envelope. The paper was made from high quality stock with her name and address written beautifully. She would know her sister's writing anywhere.

Marissa dropped the envelope onto the coffee table as she walked toward the window. She thought she heard Chad say something but she didn't respond. Instead, she shuffled the letter from one hand to the other. Until she opened it she could ignore whatever Elizabeth had to say. Good or bad. Not that she didn't love her sister, but no news was usually the best news. Elizabeth currently lived with a Pack and she was happy so there was no reason for her to write a letter when she could just call. They tried to speak on the phone every few weeks but never saw each other anymore. Marissa refused to visit and Elizabeth had a good job and a boyfriend, not allowing her to find the time to come to California.

"Here we go," Marissa muttered then tore open the back of the envelope. She pulled out the heavy card and flipped it over.

We cordially invite you…

Marissa stared at the printed words. She was doing it—finally, Elizabeth was taking a mate. When Elizabeth had moved to Texas it was because she'd met Greg. Greg was also a teacher and they both worked at a local elementary school and had been dating for several years. Marissa had known that this day would come, but she still had several emotions running through her.

She was jealous and that wasn't fair to her sister. Marissa was also happy for Elizabeth and hoped she would be able to show that.

In the ten years that they'd been separated from each other, Marissa had encouraged Elizabeth to follow her dreams, whether with her career or when she'd met Greg. Elizabeth needed to go for what she wanted, and it seemed she was finally getting what she wanted.

Just because Marissa would never have the life she craved didn't mean that she wanted Elizabeth to suffer any longer. For as long as she could remember, Elizabeth was always paying for Marissa's sins. Luckily Elizabeth had gotten away from the Pack they had been born into. Once Marissa had left, it'd opened the door to Elizabeth being accepted into another Pack.

Inside the invitation was a folded up piece of paper. Marissa opened it to find a handwritten note.

Marissa,

I know this won't be easy for you but I need you here with me to celebrate the ceremony. I won't do this without you. I know I'm asking a lot but I hope you can spend a few days with me to help me prepare and be with me when I say my vows to Greg. Don't say no. Please come.

With all my love,

Elizabeth

Well shit, how could she say no to the only thing Elizabeth had ever asked for?

"You okay?"

She jumped when Chad joined her by the window. Marissa dropped her hands but didn't let go of the letter or the invitation.

Chad nodded to her hands. "Bad news?" He'd dressed and had even put on his shoes. She guessed this was the end of their fun. Oh well, she really wasn't in the mood any longer and she had some thinking to do. Instead of answering him she only shrugged.

"I'm sorry," he said.

Then he surprised her by leaning forward and kissing her forehead. She wasn't used to such an intimate gesture. She closed her eyes for a moment to hold in the warm feeling.

"Thanks," she whispered.

"I would like to see you again," he said. "I left my number on your counter. I hope you'll call me."

She nodded, really not sure how else to respond. Maybe it wouldn't be too bad to date a human. She stayed away from relationships because she craved a shifter but had to settle for a human. It was better to just have one-night stands than not be able to give her partner one hundred percent of herself. Or that was what she'd always believed. Perhaps she needed to change her way of thinking. At least she wouldn't be alone anymore.

"Take care of yourself," he told her. "And call me."

Marissa watched as he walked away. Damn, the man really did have a nice ass. Too bad they'd gotten interrupted. With a sigh she turned back to the window. Using her heightened sight she could see the waves crashing against the sand on the shore. It was peaceful but her thoughts weren't. She had to start making plans to go to Texas next month.

Fucking Texas.

Marissa took a drink of the coffee she'd picked up at the last gas station. The hot liquid burned her tongue and tasted like sludge. It wasn't Starbucks, that was for sure, but she didn't expect any different in the middle of fucking nowhere. She had flown into Texas International Airport and rented a car to drive the rest of the way to the small town her sister called home. And small town was giving the place a lot of credit. The entire area between El Paso and the Panhandle was made up of tiny towns that even if they were combined wouldn't be as big as Dallas. There wasn't even a mall for at least another three hours. Not that she wanted to go shopping but it would be nice to have options. It was still a shock to her how excited her sister Elizabeth had been about moving here, but looking at the passing scenery of trees, trees and more trees, Marissa didn't get it. What could anyone like about the middle of nowhere? No buildings, other cars, or people around.

Rolling her window down and turning Bon Jovi even louder on the stereo, she concentrated on the drive — not the reason for coming. She dreaded going into Pack territory, but Elizabeth was the only family she had left, and, after finding her mate, Elizabeth wanted Marissa there for the mating ceremony.

That thought brought a smile to Marissa's face as she glanced at the invitation on the seat next to her. She wanted Elizabeth to be happy, and Greg sounded like a nice guy. She'd spoken to him numerous times on the phone, and he'd always been respectful toward her. And that wasn't common. A were who couldn't shift was an outsider. And everyone except Elizabeth had treated her that way her entire life.

Marissa had left the Pack she'd been raised in as soon as she could. Never to set foot in any Pack territory again. That was until later today. Elizabeth, on the other hand, had stayed until she'd met Greg, a member of a different Pack. They had met during one of the few conferences Elizabeth had attended. After the initial meeting, Greg's Pack had offered her a teaching position at the elementary school and she had taken it. He had been courting her ever since with the blessing of her new Pack Alpha, Gage Wolf.

Seriously, Elizabeth's Alpha's last name was Wolf. Could he have not come up with anything better? Maybe tried to hide what he was? Marissa just knew that Gage was going to be an arrogant, cocky, infuriating man. She was not looking forward to meeting him. Greg, however, she was actually excited to get to know.

Marissa chuckled, thinking of everything Greg had done to win her sister's heart. He'd known he'd wanted Elizabeth and had patiently waited. It had taken Elizabeth a year to agree to the mating ceremony, but she finally had. Marissa knew one of the reasons Elizabeth had been holding off was because of her. Elizabeth was a good person, and, even though Marissa had told her numerous times that Elizabeth needed to live her life as a full shifter, the guilt still hit Elizabeth.

Sometimes Marissa thought her non-shifter status was harder on her sister than herself. Marissa wasn't good enough to belong to a Pack but Elizabeth still tried to get her interested in that kind of life. It had added stress between the two of them until Marissa avoided Elizabeth's calls most of the time. That was probably why Elizabeth had gone the route of private messenger.

She hadn't meant to let so much time to go by without talking to her sister and Marissa always intended to return her messages, but life seemed to get in the way.

It didn't help that Elizabeth really didn't understand how Marissa felt about things.

Marissa had the same instincts as any other were and with that came the need for a Pack, but she had given up on that a long time ago. She'd grown up alone and would always remain that way—in the middle, between a shifter and a human. She had many gifts due to her genes—the extended lifespan, the wolf traits and some enhanced features—but not enough. Elizabeth thought Marissa could belong with her. Elizabeth was wrong and Marissa really hoped that she would concentrate on her ceremony and not nag her.

Marissa would put everything she had into this week and the ceremony that meant so much to her only sibling. Even if she would rather have been anywhere else. But she did love Elizabeth, she looked up to her sister, and had to push down the bit of jealousy that she always felt.

The differences between her and Elizabeth had grown as they had aged. That was why Marissa had never visited Elizabeth's new home. She wasn't scared of being in Pack territory, she just didn't want to face all the males and their egos. And from what she understood, the Pack's Alpha or leader, was pretty young himself.

When around other wolves, the female wolf inside her demanded that she mate with one of her own kind. So, as long as she avoided everyone except her sister as much as she could and kept her urges inside, everything would be okay. She would not act like the wolf she couldn't shift into.

And if the Alpha was anything like her old one, she'd just tell him where to stick it. The idea of telling the Alpha of a territory to go to hell made her smile wider and laugh harder. She wasn't seventeen anymore. She wasn't a scared little girl who had to follow everything someone told her. No, she was a grown woman. And she was going to enjoy the time with her sister.

She wasn't dressed to impress the Alpha or any men in the territory as she currently wore a pair of hip-hugging jeans and a tight pink T-shirt. The paint on her toenails matched the color of her shirt, as did the flip-flops. It was a far cry from the suit she wore every day as an office assistant. She felt free.

As much as she avoided being around shifter territory, her wolf craved the chance to run free. She would be on two legs instead of four but, after months inside the bustling crowded streets in a city, Marissa hoped to get a couple of private moments in the woods.

When she almost missed the turn-off to the territory gate, she jerked the wheel sharply to the left. The back of the car skidded around and kicked up dirt. Laughing, she straightened the car and slowed her speed. She didn't think Gage Wolf would be happy if she took out a couple of trees.

Why did this Pack located in the middle of nowhere need a fence and a guard station?

She reached the gate and rolled to a stop to wait for the guard. He didn't disappoint. A man over six feet came over to the window then leaned down, smiling at her.

"Can I help you?" he asked in a husky voice.

She took a deep breath and smiled back. If all the men were this good-looking, she would have her work cut out for her trying to keep her distance. They'd flirt and tease with her, and she'd have to be strong and resist, because as soon as they knew her secret, she wouldn't exist any longer to them. And no matter what she said to herself, the rejection always hurt.

"I'm Elizabeth Boyd's sister. I need directions to her house, please."

His smile didn't change and he nodded. "Give me just a minute." He winked then headed to the guard house and picked up the phone.

Marissa watched his ass flex under the tight pair of jeans he was wearing. At least as he made his call she got to enjoy the view.

The guard glanced over his shoulder at her and she waved. Yeah, she was still here and wasn't going anywhere. He was no doubt checking with the Alpha to make sure she could come in and play. With her own sister, no less, Marissa thought bitterly.

She kept her face friendly and her thoughts to herself as he came back to the car. "Problem?"

"Not at all," he said, shaking his head, and gave her directions to her sister's house. "My name's Steve if you want to get together later," he added.

Not in this life.

"Hmm, we'll see." She was careful not to commit to anything he could hold her to later. The laws of the Pack were much different from the laws where she lived. Marissa knew them all and had only ever broken one.

Shaking that unpleasant thought from her head, she drove through the gate. Looking back into the rear-view mirror, she saw Steve standing with a smile on his face.

"Down, girl," she told herself. "This is Pack territory."

The gravel crunched under her tires as Marissa made sure to keep her speed slow. She wasn't going to give anyone any reason to mess with her.

The grounds of the territory were absolutely beautiful. Thick, dark green grass went on as far as she could see. Behind a row of houses, tall and healthy trees rose up toward the sky. At least the property was pretty. Maybe she would enjoy herself just a little.

* * * *

Gage Wolf hung up the phone in his study and glanced at the clock. Elizabeth's sister had made good time. When Elizabeth had told him she wanted her sister here for the ceremony, he'd thought it was a good idea. He'd still not met the young woman but he'd asked about Elizabeth and her entire family when Greg had first brought up the option of Elizabeth joining the Pack.

He remembered the conversations he'd had with Elizabeth about her sister when he was first considering accepting Elizabeth into his Pack.

Elizabeth was protective and worried about her younger sibling. He understood it must have been hard for a non-shifter to grow up, but he didn't get why Marissa refused to see her sister.

And that, he knew, was the main reason Elizabeth had held back on the ceremony for so long. Gage was determined not to allow Marissa to hold Elizabeth back from what she wanted. And she wanted Greg.

At the knock on his door, he looked up. His second-in-command, Logan, poked his head in. "I'm taking off now."

Gage nodded.

"Want to go for a run later?" Logan asked as he opened the door wider to lean against the jamb.

"I'll be going by the Boyd house tonight," Gage told him, watching his friend and Pack member smile.

"I don't think you'll be the only one."

"What do you mean?"

The mischievous twinkle in his eyes was unmistakable. "Steve might have mentioned to a few of the guys how hot she is."

Gage shook his head. Steve hadn't wasted any time if Logan already knew. Gage didn't need further complications. "She's not here to mate."

Logan laughed. "Well, that may be beside the point."

"She doesn't need to be bothered."

"Well, who is to say it would bother her? She is a were."

"Yes, but still…" Gage wasn't sure why he already felt protective toward her. His best guess would be that Elizabeth had shared the secret of her sister not being able to shift and how it still affected her. While it wouldn't be a problem to his Pack members, he didn't want the girl overwhelmed with attention. Like most men, male shifters loved the chase of attracting a mate. They could just be more direct in their pursuit.

"Well, then you might want to get over there." With that, Logan turned and left.

Cursing, Gage stood then followed his friend down the hall. Gage cut through the living room to exit from the sliding door in the study. As the cool night air hit him, he rolled his neck and shoulders. A run would have probably been a good idea. It had only been a couple of days but he loved to shift into his other form. It gave him the freedom that he didn't get in his normal day-to-day life. All day long he was answering questions while at the same time his shifters had everything they needed. It was nice to let the wolf reign for a while. Not that he wasn't fully aware of what he was doing or his surroundings when in his shifted form. He just couldn't answer questions without the ability to speak.

Gage hurried down the curved path that would take him from the Alpha house to some of the other homes. He needed to set the ground rules down for his Pack toward this woman but first he needed to warn Marissa of the chance of having quite a few men at her tail. He hoped in the time she'd been away from her Pack and on her own that she'd found contentment. Gage worried about any ill effects from this stranger being in his territory on Elizabeth. Greg and Elizabeth deserved happiness.

Gage walked up to Elizabeth's attractive two-story house a few minutes later. Before he could ring the bell, the door opened and a young Pack member walked out onto the porch.

Gage stepped aside to let the man pass. Jeff looked surprised to see him before quickly dropping his eyes.

"Alpha."

Gage nodded his hello and strolled through the open doorway and right into the middle of a conversation in progress.

"I'm going upstairs to unpack. If you have any more visitors, tell them to come back in a week. I can't believe they all need to come by right now to congratulate you on your mating ceremony."

"That's not what this is about and you know it," Elizabeth said calmly.

"Well, I'm not a circus freak show!"

He hadn't gotten a good view of Marissa but he'd clearly heard her frustration. They really should have figured this would happen and done their best to prevent her being bombarded by eligible men.

Elizabeth stood with her back to him, her hands clasped tightly behind her, and sighed. She stiffened and he knew he'd been scented. She turned and faced Gage with a surprised look on her face.

"Gage," she greeted.

He wasn't certain if it was in welcome or not. He could practically feel the tension coming off her.

"I didn't know you were coming by. I mean, I thought you might, but with so many…" She looked nervously around her.

He only lifted an eyebrow. "I take it you've had a lot of guests?"

Elizabeth didn't appear amused. "Yeah, and it's driving her crazy. I'm sorry. I don't know where my manners are. Please come in."

Gage entered the living room, immediately taking in the new scent and the others mixed in with it. He could have named the wolves that had stopped by. There was only one smell he didn't recognize, and that had to be Elizabeth's sister.

His nostrils flared as he inhaled the fresh wood and spice smell that had his body immediately coming to life. He knew that if her scent was so alluring he was going to have his hands full keeping the available wolves away from her.

"I'll go get Marissa."

Gage laid a gentle hand on her arm. "I'll go up. I need to talk to her privately."

Elizabeth seemed uncertain for a moment, shifting on her feet and glancing upstairs.

"I just want to welcome her, tell her a few things about the ceremony, and make sure she understands some Pack rules."

Elizabeth nodded. He was sure she was worried about not only her sister but him also. Greg had mentioned the amount of stress that had been mounting.

"She... She's not always the nicest."

Elizabeth looked away when she said it, and Gage knew it wasn't easy for her to be in between her sister and her Alpha.

Gage smiled and patted her arm. "Don't worry. We'll both be fine," Gage assured her.

That seemed to console Elizabeth, and she nodded. "I'll just be in the kitchen starting dinner then."

Gage listened as he made his way upstairs. He could hear Marissa muttering to herself from down the hall.

He walked into the bedroom and stopped in his tracks. It was one of the most amazing sights he'd ever seen—her butt was sticking out from under the bed with her legs tucked under her. She moved from side to side and Gage felt himself growing hard.

He growled at the reaction, and she must have heard because there was a bang against the bottom of the bed, followed by another stream of curses.

She peered from under the bed, then crawled out, rubbing her head.

"What the hell are you doing in here?" she demanded.

"I was going to ask you the same thing. Do you always crawl under beds?"

Marissa gave him the once-over. Her attraction was immediate—he sensed it. Gage heard her heartbeat pick up and watched while she wiped her hands nervously on her pants. She shifted from foot to foot and he smelled her arousal. The stubborn look on her face told him she was going to fight it.

"Gage Wolf?"

Even though he was certain she knew exactly who he was, she'd phrased it as a question.

Gage nodded at the beauty in front of him. To say he was taken by surprise was an understatement. Where Elizabeth was pale and slender with blue eyes and blonde hair, her sister looked nothing like her.

She had long dark hair and crystal green eyes that were narrowed. It was quite obvious she didn't like her attraction to him, but he couldn't say the same. It had been a very long time since he'd felt this instant hunger.

"I am," he answered her unnecessary question. "And you are Marissa."

Marissa nodded, trying to swallow past the lump in her throat. His voice was deep and she could almost feel it wrapping around her. This reaction wasn't good and she needed to get herself under control.

He was absolutely, positively the best-looking man she had ever seen. He was taller than she was—she'd guess over six-two. He wore black slacks and a button-down shirt with the sleeves rolled up.

"Is there something you needed?" she asked, crossing her arms over her chest, feeling defensive. She was too skinny, her hair was a mess, and she was tired.

Gage followed the gesture with his eyes, and Marissa blushed when she realized she had just brought more attention to herself.

"I came to welcome you to my territory as is proper for any Pack Alpha," Gage said, taking a step closer. "And to go over some rules."

Marissa stiffened at his words, although unsurprised by them. She could guess what rules he was going to make sure she knew. She'd heard them all her life.

"You were raised in a Pack?" he asked.

Marissa nodded a second time, though he was asking a question he already had the answer to. Elizabeth had already told her that Gage was aware of her secret. Marissa had not been happy with her sister but she could understand why Elizabeth had felt it necessary to tell him.

"I don't expect things will be much different here," he said.

Marissa didn't either. "I understand," she said, stiffening her shoulders and fisting her hands at her side.

"Do you have any questions for me?"

The pep talk she had given herself on the drive allowed her to speak calmly. "No, I don't believe I have any questions about my behavior here. I assure you that I have no interest in your Pack. One week — seven days — I'll be here. I think you can deal with it as I have to. Then I'll be gone and you won't have to worry about me corrupting your precious Pack."

When she finished, something like surprise crossed his face briefly, and he growled. No one had probably ever spoken to him that way before. But Marissa wasn't going to be intimidated.

When he took a step closer, she could sense the anger and confusion from him.

"I'll warn you once about the way you talk to me. I don't know how your Alpha reacted, but that kind of disrespect will not be tolerated here."

Marissa didn't tell him that she'd never been brave enough to talk to her old Alpha like that. Marissa backed up as the Alpha stepped closer.

"Also, I know how long you are here for. I know a selfish woman like you wouldn't give up more than a week for the sister who loves her. Someone who has waited far too long to be happy because of you."

His words stopped her retreat. "Selfish? You just called me selfish."

Even with the smile that touched his lips, he didn't look any less furious. "I did."

"Well, let me tell you something, Mr. Wolf. I wouldn't be here if I didn't love my sister. I wouldn't set foot in this territory if it had not meant so much to Elizabeth. I gave my blessing to her a long time ago." Marissa took a deep breath as she wound down. She realized she was explaining herself to him and, not wanting to give him any information he could use on her later, she quickly tried to cover her outburst. "Not that it's any of your business."

Marissa backed up until she touched the wall and Gage closed the distance between them.

"You do know who I am. My status here?"

Marissa didn't trust the smooth smile or easy tone. "Yes."

"So are you trying to piss me off? Any intelligent person would know better than to tell an Alpha a Pack member wasn't his business or make the comments you have." When he reached forward and grabbed her arm, it was too fast for Marissa to avoid. "I feel sorry for the troubles you must have given to your Pack leader."

The electricity that flowed through Marissa's body at Gage's touch drew a startled breath from her. He must have felt it too, because he immediately let go of her. Marissa stared at him as neither spoke for several minutes. She grasped at anything she could say to make him go away.

"I don't have a Pack leader. But I do know how to address the Alpha of a Pack who has been kind enough to let me visit. I apologize. My attitude and disrespectful comments were uncalled for." Fear and uncertainty had her lowering her eyes to the floor in a submissive gesture. It galled her to show any submission to him, but his touch unnerved her.

She could feel his stare even though she wasn't looking at him and barely stopped herself from shuffling her feet. The urge to run coursed strongly through her body.

"I accept your apology," Gage said quietly. "I might not know everything you've been through but I do understand that you haven't always felt welcome with our kind. I expect you to tell me if you have any problems. I'll get the Pack to give you some space but you will have to interact with them."

When he'd finally spoken, she'd been so surprised that she'd lifted her eyes to meet his. Why would he even want her to talk to them? She was confused and it was really hard to concentrate, having him so close.

For a brief moment she regretted what she was. A shifter unable to change, an abomination, someone who should have been drowned at birth. She'd come to terms with it a long time ago but Gage was making her wonder what could have been if she'd been normal.

This was why she hung around with humans. They couldn't hurt her with their words and the fact that none of them would truly accept her.

"I'll be on my best behavior," she said softly. Maybe she wasn't as badass as she pretended but no one other than herself and Gage would have to know that.

"Very well then. Now, I believe your sister is downstairs about to have a fit with us up here arguing, so I suggest we finish this another time."

Marissa dipped her head in acknowledgment, relieved that he would leave now. Maybe he was just as unsettled as she was.

Gage walked out without another word to her. Marissa

sat on her bed and thought about what had just taken place. She looked up at a sound in the hall and saw Elizabeth standing at the entrance to her guest room with wide eyes and a frown.

"Don't start," Marissa warned.

Elizabeth shook her head. "Gage is a nice man and a good Alpha."

Marissa smiled even though she felt her face wanting to crack. "I'm sure he is," she lied.

More books from
Crissy Smith

Book one in the Bloodlines series

If trouble doesn't come to him, he'll find it on his own.

Book two in the Were Chronicles series

Enforcing his control never felt better

TOTALLY BOUND *What's her Secret?*

Piper's Happily Ever After
had been postponed...

*Designated
Alpha*

CRISSY
SMITH

*Piper's happily ever after has been postponed. Destiny is
funny like that.*

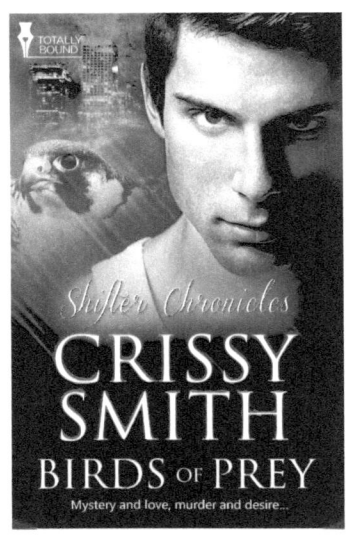

Book one in the Shifter Chronicles series

Mystery and love, murder and desire… It's going to be a rough week for the agents of the Birds of Prey shifter division.

About the Author

Crissy Smith

Crissy Smith lives in Texas with her husband, daughter, and three Labrador retrievers. The three dogs love to curl up under her computer desk and nap while she writes. It doesn't leave a lot of room for her but what's a woman to do?

When not writing or reading, she enjoys hunting, camping and shooting. But she has a girly side too and is addicted to pedicures and coffee.

She has been writing since she was a teenager and still loves everything to do with the paranormal. Her stories and characters all have a place in her heart. She loves the alpha male, the dominant werewolf, or the Master vampire which find their way in most of her books.

Learn more about the characters she has created at her website where they have their very own page. It will be updated from time to time to let you know what's going on with them. Also you can find out who will be in the next book.

Crissy Smith loves to hear from readers. You can find contact information, website details and an author profile page at https://www.totallybound.com/

Home of Erotic Romance